TALES FROM THE DARKENED STREETS OF DUBLIN

*GHOST STORIES AND TALES
OF WITCHCRAFT AND MAGIC*

BY

VARIOUS AUTHORS

British Library Cataloguing-in-Publication Data
A catalogue record for this book is available from the
British Library

CONTENTS

FIVE POUNDS OF FLESH

J. M. Synge

＊　　＊　　＊

When I was going out this morning to walk round the island with Michael, the boy who is teaching me Irish, I met an old man making his way down to the cottage. He was dressed in miserable black clothes which seemed to have come from the mainland, and was so bent with rheumatism that, at a little distance, he looked more like a spider than a human being.

Michael told me it was Pat Dirane, the storyteller old Mourteen had spoken of on the other island. I wished to turn back, as he appeared to be on his way to visit me, but Michael would not hear of it.

'He will be sitting by the fire when we come in,' he said: 'let you not be afraid, there will be time enough to be talking to him by and by.'

He was right. As I came down into the kitchen some hours later old Pat was still in the chimney-corner, blinking with the turf-smoke.

He spoke English with remarkable aptness and fluency, due, I believe, to the months he spent in the English provinces working at the harvest when he was a young man.

After a few formal compliments he told me how he had been crippled by an attack of the 'old hin' (*i.e.*, the influenza), and had been complaining ever since in addition to his rheumatism.

While the old woman was cooking my dinner he asked me if I liked stories, and offered to tell one in English, though, he added, it would be much better if I could follow the Gaelic. Then he began:

There were two farmers in County Clare. One had a son, and the other, a fine rich man, had a daughter.

The young man was wishing to marry the girl, and his father told him to try and get her if he thought well, though a power of gold would be wanting to get the like of her.

'I will try,' said the young man.

He put all his gold into a bag. Then he went over to the other farm, and threw in the gold in front of him.

'Is that all gold?' said the father of the girl.

'All gold,' said O'Conor (the young man's name was O'Conor).

'It will not weigh down my daughter,' said the father.

'We'll see that,' said O'Conor.

Then they put them in a scales, the daughter in one side and the gold in the other. The girl went down against the ground, so O'Conor took his bag and went out on the road.

As he was going along he came to where there was a little man, and he standing with his back against the wall.

'Where are you going with the bag?' said the little man.

'Going home,' said O'Conor.

'Is it gold you might be wanting?' said the man.

'It is, surely,' said O'Conor.

'I'll give you what you are wanting,' said the man, 'and we can bargain in this way—you'll pay me back in a year the gold I give you, or you'll pay me with five pounds cut off your own flesh.'

That bargain was made between them. The man gave a bag of gold to O'Conor, and he went back with it, and was married to the young woman.

They were rich people, and he built her a grand castle on the cliffs of Clare, with a window that looked out straightly over the wild ocean.

One day when he went up with his wife to look out over the wild ocean, he saw a ship coming in on the rocks, and no sails on her at all. She was wrecked on the rocks, and it was tea that was in her, and fine silk.

O'Conor and his wife went down to look at the wreck,

and when the lady O'Conor saw the silk she said she wished a dress of it.

They got the silk from the sailors, and when the Captain came up to get the money for it, O'Conor asked him to come again and take his dinner with them. They had a grand dinner, and they drank after it, and the Captain was tipsy. While they were still drinking, a letter came to O'Conor, and it was in the letter than a friend of his was dead, and that he would have to go away on a long journey. As he was getting ready the Captain came to him.

'Are you fond of your wife?' said the Captain.

'I am fond of her,' said O'Conor.

'Will you make me a bet of twenty guineas no man comes near her while you'll be away on the journey?' said the Captain.

'I will bet it,' said O'Conor, and he went away.

There was an old hag who sold small things on the road near the castle, and the lady O'Conor allowed her to sleep up in her room in a big box. The Captain went down on the road to the old hag.

'For how much will you let me sleep one night in your box?' said the Captain.

'For no money at all would I do such a thing,' said the hag.

'For ten guineas?' said the Captain.

'Not for ten guineas,' said the hag.

'For twelve guineas?' said the Captain.

'Not for twelve guineas,' said the hag.

'For fifteen guineas?' said the Captain.

'For fifteen I will do it,' said the hag.

Then she took him up and hid him in the box. When night came the lady O'Conor walked up into her room, and the Captain watched her through a hole that was in the box. He saw her take off her two rings and put them on a kind of board that was over her head like a chimney-piece, and take off her clothes, except her shift, and go up into her bed.

As soon as she was asleep the Captain came out of his box, and he had some means of making a light, for he lit the candle. He went over to the bed where she was sleeping without disturbing her at all, or doing any bad thing, and he took the two rings off the board, and blew out the light, and went down again into the box.

He paused for a moment, and a deep sigh of relief rose from the men and women who had crowded in while the story was going on, till the kitchen was filled with people.

As the Captain was coming out of his box the girls, who had appeared to know no English, stopped their spinning and held their breath with expectation.

The old man went on—

When O'Conor came back the Captain met him, and

told him that he had been a night in his wife's room, and gave him the two rings.

O'Conor gave him the twenty guineas of the bet. Then he went up into the castle, and he took his wife up to look out of the window over the wild ocean. While she was looking he pushed her from behind, and she fell down over the cliff into the sea.

An old woman was on the shore, and she saw her falling. She went down then to the surf and pulled her out all wet and in great disorder, and she took the wet clothes off of her, and put on some old rags belonging to herself.

When O'Conor had pushed his wife from the window he went away into the land.

After a while the lady O'Conor went out searching for him, and when she had gone here and there a long time in the country, she heard that he was reaping in a field with sixty men.

She came to the field and she wanted to go in, but the gate-man would not open the gate for her. Then the owner came by, and she told him her story. He brought her in, and her husband was there, reaping, but he never gave any sign of knowing her. She showed him to the owner, and he made the man come out and go with his wife.

Then the lady O'Conor took him out on the road where there were horses, and they rode away.

When they came to the place where O'Conor had met the little man, he was there on the road before them.

'Have you my gold on you?' said the man.

'I have not,' said O'Conor.

'Then you'll pay me the flesh off your body,' said the man.

They went into a house, and a knife was brought, and a clean white cloth was put on the table, and O'Conor was put upon the cloth.

Then the little man was going to strike the lancet into him, when says lady O'Conor—

'Have you bargained for five pounds of flesh?'

'For five pounds of flesh,' said the man.

'Have you bargained for any drop of his blood?' said lady O'Conor.

'For no blood,' said the man.

'Cut out the flesh,' said lady O'Conor, 'but if you spill one drop of his blood I'll put that through you.' And she put a pistol to his head.

The little man went away, and they saw no more of him.

When they got home to their castle they made a great supper, and they invited the Captain and the old hag, and the old woman that had pulled the lady O'Conor out of the sea.

After they had eaten well the lady O'Conor began, and

she said they would all tell their stories. Then she told how she had been saved from the sea, and how she had found her husband.

Then the old woman told her story, the way she had found the lady O'Conor wet, and in great disorder, and had brought her in and put on her some old rags of her own.

The lady O'Conor asked the Captain for his story, but he said they would get no story from him. Then she took her pistol out of her pocket, and she put it on the edge of the table, and she said that any one that would not tell his story would get a bullet into him.

Then the Captain told the way he had got into the box, and come over to her bed without touching her at all, and had taken away the rings.

Then the lady O'Conor took the pistol and shot the hag through the body, and they threw her over the cliff into the sea.

NARRATIVE OF THE GHOST
OF A HAND

J. Sheridan de Fanu

I'm sure she believed every word she related, for old Sally was veracious. But all this was worth just so much as such talk commonly is—marvels, fabulae, what our ancestors called winter's tales—which gathered details from every narrator, and dilated in the act of narration. Still it was not quite for nothing that the house was held to be haunted. Under all this smoke there smouldered just a little spark of truth—an authenticated mystery, for the solution of which some of my readers may possibly suggest a theory, though I confess I can't.

Miss Rebecca Chattesworth, in a letter dated late in the autumn of 1753, gives a minute and curious relation of occurrences in the Tiled House, which, it is plain, although at starting she protests against all such fooleries, she has heard with a peculiar sort of interest, and relates it certainly with an awful sort of particularity.

I was for printing the entire letter, which is really very singular as well as characteristic. But my publisher meets me with his *veto*; and I believe he is right. The worthy old lady's letter *is*, perhaps, too long ; and I must rest content with a few hungry notes of its tenor.

That year, and somewhere about the 24th October, there broke out a strange dispute between Mr. Alderman Harper, of High Street, Dublin, and my Lord Castlemallard, who, in virtue of his cousinship to the young heir's mother, had undertaken for him the management of the tiny estate on which the Tiled or Tyled House—for I find it spelt both ways—stood.

This Alderman Harper had agreed for a lease of the house for his daughter, who was married to a gentleman named Prosser. He furnished it and put up hangings, and otherwise went to considerable expense. Mr. and Mrs. Prosser came there sometime in June, and after having parted with a good many servants in the interval, she made up her mind that she could not live in the house, and her father waited on Lord Castlemallard, and told him plainly that he would not take out the lease because the house was subjected to annoyances which he could not explain. In plain terms, he said it was haunted, and that no servants would live there more than a few weeks, and that after what his son-in-law's family had suffered there, not only should he be excused from taking a lease of it, but that the house itself ought to be pulled down as a nuisance and the habitual haunt of something worse than human malefactors.

Lord Castlemallard filed a bill in the Equity side of the Exchequer to compel Mr. Alderman Harper to perform his contract, by taking out the lease. But the Alderman drew an answer, supported by no less than seven long affidavits, copies of all which were furnished to his lordship, and with the desired effect ; for rather than compel him to place them upon the file of the court, his lordship struck, and consented to release him.

I am sorry the cause did not proceed at least far enough to place upon the files of the court the very authentic and unaccountable story which Miss Rebecca relates.

The annoyances described did not begin till the end of August, when, one evening, Mrs. Prosser, quite alone, was sitting in the twilight at the back parlour window, which was open, looking out into the orchard, and plainly saw a hand stealthily placed upon the stone window-sill outside, as if by some one beneath the window, at her right side, intending to climb up. There was nothing but the hand, which was rather short but handsomely formed, and white and plump, laid on the edge of the window-sill ; and it was not a very young hand, but one aged, somewhere about forty, as she conjectured. It was only a few weeks before that the horrible robbery at Clondalkin had taken place, and the lady fancied that the hand was that of one of the miscreants who was now about to scale the windows of the Tiled House. She uttered a loud scream and an ejaculation of terror, and at the same moment the hand was quietly withdrawn.

Search was made in the orchard, but no indications of any person's having been under the window, beneath which, ranged along the wall, stood a great column of flower-pots, which it seemed must have prevented any one's coming within reach of it.

The same night there came a hasty tapping, every now and then, at the window of the kitchen. The women grew frightened, and the servant-man, taking fire-arms with him, opened the back-door, but discovered nothing. As he shut it, however, he said, "a thump came on it," and a pressure as of somebody striving to force his way in, which frightened *him*; and though the tapping went on upon the kitchen window panes, he made no further explorations.

About six o'clock on the Saturday evening following, the cook, "an honest, sober woman, now aged nigh sixty years," being alone in the kitchen, saw, on looking up, it is supposed, the same fat but aristocratic-looking hand, laid with its palm against the glass, near the side of the window, and this time moving slowly up and down, pressed all the while against the glass, as if feeling carefully for some inequality in its surface. She cried out, and said something like a prayer on seeing it. But it was not withdrawn for several seconds after.

After this, for a great many nights, there came at first a low, and afterwards an angry rapping, as it seemed with a set of clenched knuckles at the back-door. And the servant-man would not open it, but called to know who was there; and there came no answer, only a sound as if the palm of the hand was placed against it, and drawn slowly from side to side with a sort of soft, groping motion.

All this time, sitting in the back parlour, which, for the time, they used as a drawing-room, Mr. and Mrs. Prosser were disturbed by rappings at the window, sometimes very low and furtive, like a clandestine signal, and at others sudden and so loud as to threaten the breaking of the pane.

This was all at the back of the house, which looked upon the orchard as you know. But on a Tuesday night, at about half-past nine, there came precisely the same rapping at the hall-door, and went on, to the great annoyance of the master and terror of his wife, at intervals, for nearly two hours.

After this, for several days and nights, they had no annoyance whatsoever, and began to think that the nuisance had expended itself. But on the night of the 13th September, Jane Easterbrook, an English maid, having gone into the pantry for the small silver bowl in which her mistress's posset was served, happening to look up at the little window of only four panes, observed through an augur-hole which was drilled through the window frame, for the admission of a bolt to secure the shutter, a white pudgy finger—first the tip, and then the two first joints introduced, and turned about this way and that, crooked against the inside, as if in search of a fastening which its owner designed to push aside. When the maid got back into the kitchen, we are told "she fell into 'a swounde,' and was all the next day very weak."

Mr. Prosser being, I've heard, a hard-headed and conceited sort of fellow, scouted the ghost, and sneered at the fears of his family. He was privately of opinion that the whole affair was a practical joke or a fraud, and waited an opportunity of catching the rogue *flagrante delicto*. He did not long keep this theory to himself, but let it out by degrees with no stint of oaths and threats, believing that some domestic traitor held the thread of the conspiracy.

Indeed it was time something were done; for not only his servants, but good Mrs. Prosser herself, had grown to look unhappy and anxious. They kept at home from the hour of sunset, and would not venture about the house after nightfall, except in couples.

The knocking had ceased for about a week; when one night, Mrs. Prosser being in the nursery, her husband, who was in the parlour, heard it begin very softly at the hall-door.

The air was quite still, which favoured his hearing distinctly. This was the first time there had been any disturbance at that side of the house, and the character of the summons was changed.

Mr. Prosser, leaving the parlour-door open, it seems, went quietly into the hall. The sound was that of beating on the outside of the stout door, softly and regularly, "with the flat of the hand." He was going to open it suddenly, but changed his mind; and went back very quietly, and on to the head of the kitchen stair, where was a "strong closet" over the pantry, in which he kept his firearms, swords, and canes.

Here he called his man-servant, whom he believed to be honest, and, with a pair of loaded pistols in his own coat-pockets, and giving another pair to him, he went as lightly as he could, followed by the man, and with a stout walking-cane in his hand, forward to the door.

Everything went as Mr. Prosser wished. The besieger of his house, so far from taking fright at their approach, grew more impatient; and the sort of patting which had aroused his attention at first assumed the rhythm and emphasis of a series of double-knocks.

Mr. Prosser, angry, opened the door with his right arm across, cane in hand. Looking, he saw nothing; but his arm was jerked up oddly, as it might be with the hollow of a hand, and something passed under it, with a kind of gentle squeeze. The servant neither saw nor felt anything, and did not know why his master looked back so hastily, cutting with his cane, and shutting the door with so sudden a slam.

From that time Mr. Prosser discontinued his angry talk and swearing about it, and seemed nearly as averse from the subject as the rest of his family. He grew, in fact, very uncomfortable, feeling an inward persuasion that when, in answer to the summons, he had opened the hall-door, he had actually given ad mission to the besieger.

He said nothing to Mrs. Prosser, but went up earlier to his bedroom, "where he read a while in his Bible, and said his prayers." I hope the particular relation of this circumstance does not indicate its singularity. He lay awake a good while, it appears; and, as he supposed, about a quarter past twelve he heard the soft palm of a hand patting on the outside of the bedroom-door, and then brushed slowly along it.

Up bounced Mr. Prosser, very much frightened, and locked the door, crying, "Who's there?" but receiving no answer, but the same brushing sound of a soft hand drawn over the panels, which he knew only too well.

In the morning the housemaid was terrified by the impression of a hand in the dust of the "little parlour" table, where they had been unpacking delft and other things the day before. The print of the naked foot in the sea-sand did not frighten Robinson Crusoe half so much. They were by this time all nervous, and some of them half-crazed, about the hand.

Mr. Prosser went to examine the mark, and, made light of it, but, as he swore afterwards, rather to quiet his servants than from any comfortable feeling about it in his own mind; however, he had them all, one by one, into the room, and made each place his or her hand, palm downward, on the same table, thus taking a similar impression from every person in the house, including himself and his wife; and his "affidavit" deposed that the formation of the hand so impressed differed altogether from those of the living inhabitants of the house, and corresponded with that of the hand seen by Mrs. Prosser and by the cook.

Whoever or whatever the owner of that hand might be, they all felt this subtle demonstration to mean that it was declared he was no longer out of doors, but had established himself in the house.

And now Mrs. Prosser began to be troubled with strange and horrible dreams, some of which as set out in detail, in Aunt Rebecca's long letter, are really very appalling nightmares. But one night, as Mr. Prosser closed his bedchamber-door, he was struck somewhat by the utter silence of the room, there being no sound of breathing, which seemed unaccountable to him, as he knew his wife was in bed, and his ears were particularly sharp.

There was a candle burning on a small table at the foot of the bed, besides the one he held in one hand, a heavy ledger, connected with his father-in-law's business being under his arm. He drew the curtain at the side of the bed, and saw Mrs. Prosser lying, as for a few seconds he mortally feared, dead, her face being motionless, white, and covered with a cold dew; and on the pillow, close beside her head, and just within the curtains, was, as he first thought, a toad—but really the same fattish hand, the wrist resting on the pillow, and the fingers extended towards her temple.

Mr. Prosser, with a horrified jerk, pitched the ledger right at the curtains, behind which the owner of the hand might be supposed to stand. The hand was instantaneously and smoothly snatched away, the curtains made a great wave, and Mr. Prosser got round the bed in time to see the closet-door, which was at the other side, pulled to by the same white, puffy hand, as he believed.

He drew the door open with a fling, and stared in: but the closet was empty, except for the clothes hanging from the pegs on the wall, and the dressing-table and looking-glass facing the windows. He shut it sharply, and locked it, and felt for a minute, he says, "as if he were like to lose his wits"; then, ringing at the bell, he brought the servants, and with much ado they recovered Mrs. Prosser from a sort of "trance," in which, he says, from her looks, she seemed to have suffered "the pains of death": and Aunt Rebecca adds, "from what she told me of her visions, with her own lips, he might have added, 'and of hell also.'"

But the occurrence which seems to have determined the crisis was the strange sickness of their eldest child, a little boy aged between two and three years. He lay awake, seemingly in paroxysms of terror, and the doctors who were called in, set down the symptoms to incipient water on the brain. Mrs. Prosser used to sit up with the nurse, by the nursery fire, much troubled in mind about the condition of her child.

His bed was placed sideways along the wall, with its head against the door of a press or cupboard, which, however did not shut quite close. There was a little valance, about a foot deep, round the top of the child's bed, and this descended within some ten or twelve inches of the pillow on which it lay.

They observed that the little creature was quieter whenever they took it up and held it on their laps. They had just replaced him, as he seemed to have grown quite sleepy and tranquil, but he was not five minutes in his bed when he began to scream in one of his frenzies of terror; at the same moment the nurse, for the first time, detected, and Mrs. Prosser equally plainly saw, following the direction of *her* eyes, the real cause of the child's sufferings.

Protruding through the aperture of the press, and shrouded

in the shade of the valance, they plainly saw the white fat hand, palm downwards, presented towards the head of the child. The mother uttered a scream, and snatched the child from its little bed, and she and the nurse ran down to the lady's sleeping-room, where Mr. Prosser was in bed, shutting the door as they entered; and they had hardly done so, when a gentle tap came to it from the outside.

There is a great deal more, but this will suffice. The singularity of the narrative seems to me to be this, that it describes the ghost of a hand, and no more. The person to whom that hand belonged never once appeared; nor was it a hand separated from a body, but only a hand so manifested and introduced that its owner was always, by some crafty accident, hidden from view.

In the year 1819, at a college breakfast, I met a Mr. Prosser—a thin, grave, but rather chatty old gentleman, with very white hair drawn back into a pigtail—and he told us all, with a concise particularity, a story of his cousin, James Prosser, who, when an infant, had slept for some time in what his mother said was a haunted nursery in an old house near Chapelizod, and who, whenever he was ill, over-fatigued, or in anywise feverish, suffered all through his life as he had done from a time he could scarce remember, from a vision of a certain gentleman, fat and pale, every curl of whose wig, every button and fold of whose laced clothes, and every feature and line of whose sensual, benignant, and unwholesome face, was as minutely engraven upon his memory as the dress and lineaments of his own grandfather's portrait, which hung before him every day at breakfast, dinner, and supper.

Mr. Prosser mentioned this as an instance of a curiously monotonous, individualised, and persistent nightmare, and hinted the extreme horror and anxiety with which his cousin, of whom he spoke in the past tense as "poor Jemmie," was at any time induced to mention it.

I hope the reader will pardon me for loitering so long in the Tiled House, but this sort of lore has always had a charm for me; and people, you know, especially old people, will talk of what most interests themselves, too often forgetting that others may have had more than enough of it.

AN ACCOUNT OF SOME
STRANGE DISTURBANCES
IN AUNGIER STREET

J. Sheridan Le Fanu

It is not worth telling, this story of mine—at least, not worth writing. Told, indeed, as I have sometimes been called upon to tell it, to a circle of intelligent and eager faces, lighted up by a good after-dinner fire on a winter's evening, with a cold wind rising and wailing outside, and all snug and cosy within, it has gone off—though I say it, who should not—indifferent well. But it is a venture to do as you would have me. Pen, ink, and paper are cold vehicles for the marvellous, and a "reader" decidedly a more critical animal than a "listener." If, however, you can induce your friends to read it after nightfall, and when the fireside talk has run for a while on thrilling tales of shapeless terror; in short, if you will secure me the *mollia tempora fandi*, I will go to my work, and say my say, with better heart. Well, then, these conditions presupposed, I shall waste no more words, but tell you simply how it all happened.

My cousin (Tom Ludlow) and I studied medicine together. I think he would have succeeded, had he stuck to the profession; but he preferred the Church, poor fellow, and died early, a sacrifice to contagion, contracted in the noble discharge of his duties. For my present purpose, I say enough of his character when I mention that he was of a sedate but frank and cheerful nature; very exact in his observance of truth, and not by any means like myself—of an excitable or nervous temperament.

My Uncle Ludlow—Tom's father—while we were attending lectures, purchased three or four old houses in Aungier Street, one of which was unoccupied. *He* resided in the country, and Tom proposed that we should take up our abode in the untenanted house, so long as it should continue unlet; a move which would accomplish the double end of settling us nearer alike to our lecture-rooms and to our amusements, and of relieving us from the weekly charge of rent for our lodgings.

Our furniture was very scant—our whole equipage remarkably modest and primitive; and, in short, our arrangements pretty nearly as simple as those of a bivouac. Our new plan was, therefore, executed almost as soon as conceived. The front drawing-room was our sitting-room. I had the bedroom over it, and Tom the back bedroom on the same floor, which nothing could have induced me to occupy.

The house, to begin with, was a very old one. It had been, I believe, newly fronted about fifty years before; but with this exception, it had nothing modern about it. The agent who bought it and looked into the titles for my uncle, told me that it was sold, along with much other forfeited property, at Chichester House, I think, in 1702; and had belonged to Sir Thomas Hacket, who was Lord Mayor of Dublin in James II's time. How old it was *then*, I can't say; but, at all events, it had seen years and changes enough to have contracted all that mysterious and saddened air, at once exciting and depressing, which belongs to most old mansions.

There had been very little done in the way of modernising details; and, perhaps, it was better so; for there was something queer and by-gone in the very walls and ceilings—in the shape of doors and windows—in the odd diagonal site of the chimney-pieces—in the beams and ponderous cornices—not to mention the singular solidity of all the woodwork, from the banisters to the window-frames, which hopelessly defied disguise, and would have emphatically proclaimed their antiquity through any conceivable amount of modern finery and varnish.

An effort had, indeed, been made, to the extent of papering the drawing-rooms; but, somehow the paper looked raw and out of keeping; and the old woman, who kept a little dirt-pie of a shop in the lane, and whose daughter—a girl of two and fifty—was our solitary handmaid, coming in at sunrise, and chastely receding again as soon as she had made all ready for tea in our state apartment;—this woman, I say, remembered it, when old Judge Horrocks (who, having earned the reputation of a particularly "hanging judge," ended by hanging himself, as the coroner's jury found, under an impulse of "temporary insanity," with a child's skipping-rope, over the massive old banisters) resided there, entertaining good company, with fine venison and rare old port. In those halcyon days, the drawing-rooms were hung with gilded leather, and, I dare say, cut a good figure, for they were really spacious rooms.

The bedrooms were wainscoted, but the front one was not gloomy; and in it the cosiness of antiquity quite overcame its sombre associations. But the back bedroom, with its two queerly-placed melancholy windows, staring vacantly at the foot of the bed, and with the shadowy recess to be found in most old houses in Dublin, like a large ghostly closet, which, from congeniality of temperament, had amalgamated with the bedchamber, and dissolved the partition. At night-time, this "alcove"—as our "maid" was wont to call it—had, in my eyes, a specially sinister and suggestive character. Tom's distant and solitary candle glimmered vainly into its darkness. *There* it was always overlooking him—always itself impenetrable. But this was only part of the effect. The whole room was, I can't tell how, repulsive to me. There was, I suppose, in its proportions and features, a latent discord—a certain mysterious and indescribable relation, which jarred indistinctly upon some secret sense of the fitting and the safe, and raised indefinable suspicions and apprehensions of the imagination. On the whole, as I began by saying, nothing could have induced me to pass a night alone in it.

I had never pretended to conceal from poor Tom my superstitious weakness; and he, on the other hand, most unaffectedly ridiculed my tremors. The sceptic was, however, destined to receive a lesson, as you shall hear.

We had not been very long in occupation of our respective dormitories, when I began to complain of uneasy nights and disturbed sleep. I was, I suppose, the more impatient under this annoyance, as I was usually a sound sleeper, and by no means prone to nightmares. It was now, however, my destiny, instead of enjoying my customary repose, every night to "sup full of horrors." After a preliminary course of disagreeable and frightful dreams, my troubles took a definite form, and the same vision, without an appreciable variation in a single detail, visited me at least (on an average) every second night in the week.

Now, this dream, nightmare, or infernal illusion—which

you please—of which I was the miserable sport, was on this wise:—

I saw, or thought I saw, with the most abominable distinctness, although at the time in profound darkness, every article of furniture and accidental arrangement of the chamber in which I lay. This, as you know, is incidental to ordinary nightmare. Well, while in this clairvoyant condition, which seemed but the lighting up of the theatre in which was to be exhibited the monotonous tableau of horror, which made my nights insupportable, my attention invariably became, I know not why, fixed upon the windows opposite the foot of my bed; and, uniformly with the same effect, a sense of dreadful anticipation always took slow but sure possession of me. I became somehow conscious of a sort of horrid but undefined preparation going forward in some unknown quarter, and by some unknown agency, for my torment; and, after an interval, which always seemed to me of the same length, a picture suddenly flew up to the window, where it remained fixed, as if by an electrical attraction, and my discipline of horror then commenced, to last perhaps for hours. The picture thus mysteriously glued to the window-panes, was the portrait of an old man, in a crimson flowered silk dressing-gown, the folds of which I could now describe, with a countenance embodying a strange mixture of intellect, sensuality, and power, but withal sinister and full of malignant omen. His nose was hooked, like the beak of a vulture; his eyes large, grey, and prominent, and lighted up with a more than mortal cruelty and coldness. These features were surmounted by a crimson velvet cap, the hair that peeped from under which was white with age, while the eyebrows retained their original blackness. Well I remember every line, hue, and shadow of that stony countenance, and well I may! The gaze of this hellish visage was fixed upon me, and mine returned it with the inexplicable fascination of nightmare, for what appeared to me to be hours of agony. At last—

"*The cock he crew, away then flew*"

the fiend who had enslaved me through the awful watches of the night; and, harassed and nervous, I rose to the duties of the day.

I had—I can't say exactly why, but it may have been from the exquisite anguish and profound impressions of unearthly horror, with which this strange phantasmagoria was associated—an insurmountable antipathy to describing the exact nature of my nightly troubles to my friend and comrade. Generally, however, I told him that I was haunted by abominable dreams; and, true to the imputed materialism of medicine, we put our heads together to dispel my horrors, not by exorcism, but by a tonic.

I will do this tonic justice, and frankly admit that the

accursed portrait began to intermit its visits under its influence. What of that? Was this singular apparition—as full of character as of terror—therefore the creature of my fancy, or the invention of my poor stomach? Was it, in short, *subjective* (to borrow the technical slang of the day) and not the palpable aggression and intrusion of an external agent? That, good friend, as we will both admit, by no means follows. The evil spirit, who enthralled my senses in the shape of that portrait, may have been just as near me, just as energetic, just as malignant, though I saw him not. What means the whole moral code of revealed religion regarding the due keeping of our own bodies, soberness, temperance, etc.? here is an obvious connexion between the material and the invisible; the healthy tone of the system, and its unimpaired energy, may, for aught we can tell, guard us against influences which would otherwise render life itself terrific. The mesmerist and the electro-biologist will fail upon an average with nine patients out of ten—so may the evil spirit. Special conditions of the corporeal system are indispensable to the production of certain spiritual phenomena. The operation succeeds sometimes—sometimes fails—that is all.

I found afterwards that my would-be sceptical companion had his troubles too. But of these I knew nothing yet. One night, for a wonder, I was sleeping soundly, when I was roused by a step on the lobby outside my room, followed by the loud clang of what turned out to be a large brass candlestick, flung with all his force by poor Tom Ludlow over the banisters, and rattling with a rebound down the second flight of stairs; and almost concurrently with this, Tom burst open my door, and bounced into my room backwards, in a state of extraordinary agitation.

I had jumped out of bed and clutched him by the arm before I had any distinct idea of my own whereabouts. There we were—in our shirts—standing before the open door—staring through the great old banister opposite, at the lobby window, through which the sickly light of a clouded moon was gleaming.

"What's the matter, Tom? What's the matter with you? What the devil's the matter with you, Tom?" I demanded, shaking him with nervous impatience.

He took a long breath before he answered me, and then it was not very coherently.

"It's nothing, nothing at all—did I speak?—what did I say?—where's the candle, Richard? It's dark; I—I had a candle!"

"Yes, dark enough," I said; "but what's the matter?—what *is* it?—why don't you speak, Tom?—have you lost your wits?—what is the matter?"

"The matter?—oh, it is all over. It must have been a dream—nothing at all but a dream—don't you think so? It could not be anything more than a dream."

"Of *course*," said I, feeling uncommonly nervous, "it *was* a dream."

"I thought," he said, "there was a man in my room, and—and I jumped out of bed; and—and—where's the candle?"

"In your room, most likely," I said, "shall I go and bring it?"

"No; stay here—don't go; it's no matter—don't, I tell you; it was all a dream. Bolt the door, Dick; I'll stay here with you—I feel nervous. So, Dick, like a good fellow, light your candle and open the window—I am in a *shocking state*."

I did as he asked me, and robing himself like Granuaile in one of my blankets, he seated himself close beside my bed.

Everybody knows how contagious is fear of all sorts, but more especially that particular kind of fear under which poor Tom was at that moment labouring. I would not have heard, nor I believe would he have recapitulated, just at that moment, for half the world, the details of the hideous vision which had so unmanned him.

"Don't mind telling me anything about your nonsenical dream, Tom," said I, affecting contempt, really in a panic; "let us talk about something else; but it is quite plain that this dirty old house disagrees with us both, and hang me if I stay here any longer, to be pestered with indigestion and—and—bad nights, so we may as well look out for lodgings—

don't you think so?—at once."

Tom agreed, and, after an interval, said—

"I have been thinking, Richard, that it is a long time since I saw my father, and I have made up my mind to go down tomorrow and return in a day or two, and you can take rooms for us in the meantime."

I fancied that this resolution, obviously the result of the vision which had so profoundly scared him, would probably vanish next morning with the damps and shadows of night. But I was mistaken. Off went Tom at peep of day to the country, having agreed that so soon as I had secured suitable lodgings, I was to recall him by letter from his visit to my Uncle Ludlow.

Now, anxious as I was to change my quarters, it so happened, owing to a series of petty procrastinations and accidents, that nearly a week elapsed before my bargain was made and my letter of recall on the wing to Tom; and, in the meantime, a trifling adventure or two had occurred to your humble servant, which, absurd as they now appear, diminished by distance, did certainly at the time serve to whet my appetite for change considerably.

A night or two after the departure of my comrade, I was sitting by my bedroom fire, the door locked, and the ingredients of a tumbler of hot whisky-punch upon the crazy spider-table; for, as the best mode of keeping the

"Black spirits and white,
Blue spirits and grey,"

with which I was environed, at bay, I had adopted the practice recommended by the wisdom of my ancestors, and "kept my spirits up by pouring spirits down." I had thrown aside my volume of Anatomy, and was treating myself by way of a tonic, preparatory to my punch and bed, to half-a-dozen pages of the *Spectator*, when I heard a step on the flight of stairs descending from the attics. It was two o'clock, and the streets were as silent as a churchyard—the sounds were, therefore, perfectly distinct. There was a slow, heavy tread, characterised by the emphasis and deliberation of age, descending by the narrow staircase from above; and, what made the sound more singular, it was plain that the feet which produced it were perfectly bare, measuring the descent with something between a pound and a flop, very ugly to hear.

I knew quite well that my attendant had gone away many hours before, and that nobody but myself had any business in the house. It was quite plain also that the person who was coming downstairs had no intention whatever of concealing his movements; but, on the contrary, appeared disposed to make even more noise, and proceed more deliberately, than was at all necessary. When the step reached the foot of the stairs outside my room, it seemed to stop; and I expected every moment to see my door open spontaneously, and give admission to the original of my detested portrait. I was, however, relieved in a few seconds by hearing the descent renewed, just in the same manner, upon the staircase leading down to the drawing-rooms, and thence, after another pause, down the next flight, and so on to the hall, whence I heard no more.

Now, by the time the sound had ceased, I was wound up, as they say, to a very unpleasant pitch of excitement. I listened, but there was not a stir. I screwed up my courage to a decisive experiment—opened my door, and in a stentorian voice bawled over the banisters, "Who's there?" There was no answer, but the ringing of my own voice through the empty old house,—no renewal of the movement; nothing, in short, to give my unpleasant sensations a definite direction. There is, I think, something most disagreeably disenchanting in the sound of one's own voice under such circumstances, exerted in solitude and in vain. It redoubled my sense of isolation, and my misgivings increased on perceiving that the door, which I certainly thought I had left open, was closed behind me; in a vague alarm, lest my retreat should be cut off, I got again into my room as quickly as I could, where I remained in a state of imaginary blockade, and very uncomfortable indeed, till morning.

Next night brought no return of my barefooted fellow-lodger; but the night following, being in my bed, and in the dark—somewhere, I suppose, about the same hour as before, I distinctly heard the old fellow again descending from the garrets.

This time I had had my punch, and the *morale* of the garrison was consequently excellent. I jumped out of bed, clutched the poker as I passed the expiring fire, and in a moment was upon the lobby. The sound had ceased by this time—the dark and chill were discouraging; and, guess my horror, when I saw, or thought I saw, a black monster, whether in the shape of a man or a bear I could not say, standing, with its back to the wall, on the lobby, facing me, with a pair of great greenish eyes shining dimly out. Now, I must be frank, and confess that the cupboard which displayed our plates and cups stood just there, though at the moment I did not recollect it. At the same time I must honestly say, that making every allowance for an excited imagination, I never could satisfy myself that I was made the dupe of my own fancy in this matter; for this apparition, after one or two shiftings of shape, as if in the act of incipient transformation, began, as it seemed on second thoughts, to advance upon me in its original form. From an instinct of terror rather than of courage, I hurled the poker, with all my force, at its head; and to the music of a horrid crash made my way into my room, and double-locked the door. Then, in a minute more, I heard the horrid bare feet walk down the stairs, till the sound ceased in the hall, as on the former occasion.

If the apparition of the night before was an ocular delusion of my fancy sporting with the dark outlines of our cupboard, and if its horrid eyes were nothing but a pair of inverted teacups, I had, at all events, the satisfaction of having launched the poker with admirable effect, and in true "fancy" phrase, "knocked its two daylights into one," as the commingled fragments of my tea-service testified. I did my best to gather comfort and courage from these evidences; but it would not do. And then what could I say of those horrid bare feet, and the regular tramp, tramp, tramp, which measured the distance of the entire staircase through the solitude of my haunted dwelling, and at an hour when no good influence was stirring? Confound it!—the whole affair was abominable. I was out of spirits, and dreaded the approach of night.

It came, ushered ominously in with a thunder-storm and dull torrents of depressing rain. Earlier than usual the streets grew silent; and by twelve o'clock nothing but the comfortless pattering of the rain was to be heard.

I made myself as snug as I could. I lighted *two* candles instead of one. I forswore bed, and held myself in readiness for a sally, candle in hand; for, *coute qui coute*, I was resolved to *see* the being, if visible at all, who troubled the nightly stillness of my mansion. I was fidgety and nervous and, tried in vain to interest myself with my books. I walked up and down my room, whistling in turn martial and hilarious music, and listening ever and anon for the dreaded noise. I sate down and stared at the square label on the solemn and reserved-looking black botde, until "FLANAGAN & Co.'s BEST OLD MALT WHISKY" grew into a sort of subdued accompaniment to all the fantastic and horrible speculations which chased one another through my brain.

Silence, meanwhile, grew more silent, and darkness darker. I listened in vain for the rumble of a vehicle, or the dull clamour of a distant row. There was nothing but the sound of a rising wind, which had succeeded the thunderstorm that had travelled over the Dublin mountains quite out of hearing. In the middle of this great city I began to feel myself alone with nature, and Heaven knows what beside. My courage was ebbing. Punch, however, which makes beasts of so many, made a man of me again—just in time to hear with tolerable nerve and firmness the lumpy, flabby, naked feet deliberately descending the stairs again.

I took a candle, not without a tremor. As I crossed the floor I tried to extemporise a prayer, but stopped short to listen, and never finished it. The steps continued. I confess I hesitated for some seconds at the door before I took heart of grace and opened it. When I peeped out the lobby was perfectly empty—there was no monster standing on the staircase; and as the detested sound ceased, I was reassured enough to venture forward nearly to the banisters. Horror of horrors! within a stair or two beneath the spot where I stood the unearthly tread smote the floor. My eye caught something in motion; it was about the size of Goliath's foot—it was grey, heavy, and flapped with a dead weight from one step to another. As I am alive, it was the most monstrous grey rat I ever beheld or imagined.

Shakespeare says—"Some men there are cannot abide a gaping pig, and some that are mad if they behold a cat." I went well-nigh out of my wits when I beheld this *rat*; for, laugh at me as you may, it fixed upon me, I thought, a perfectly human expression of malice; and, as it shuffled about and looked up into my face almost from between my feet, I saw, I could swear it—I felt it then, and know it now, the infernal gaze and the accursed countenance of my old friend in the portrait, transfused into the visage of the bloated vermin before me.

I bounced into my room again with a feeling of loathing and horror I cannot describe, and locked and bolted my door as if a lion had been at the other side. D——n him or *it*; curse the portrait and its original! I felt in my soul that the rat—yes, the *rat*, the RAT I had just seen, was that evil being in masquerade, and rambling through the house upon some infernal night lark.

Next morning I was early trudging through the miry streets; and, among other transactions, posted a peremptory note recalling Tom. On my return, however, I found a note from my absent "chum," announcing his intended return next day. I was doubly rejoiced at this, because I had succeeded in getting rooms; and because the change of scene and return of my comrade were rendered specially pleasant by the last night's half ridiculous half horrible adventure.

I slept extemporaneously in my new quarters in Digges' Street that night, and next morning returned for breakfast to the haunted mansion, where I was certain Tom would call immediately on his arrival.

I was quite right—he came; and almost his first question referred to the primary object of our change of residence.

"Thank God," he said with genuine fervour, on hearing that all was arranged. "On *your* account I am delighted. As to myself, I assure you that no earthly consideration could have induced me ever again to pass a night in this disastrous old house."

"Confound the house!" I ejaculated, with a genuine mixture of fear and detestation, "we have not had a pleasant hour since we came to live here"; and so I went on, and related incidentally my adventure with the plethoric old rat.

"Well, if that were *all*," said my cousin, affecting to make light of the matter, "I don't think I should have minded it very much."

"Ay, but its eye—its countenance, my dear Tom," urged I; "if you had seen *that*, you would have felt it might be *anything* but what it seemed."

"I am inclined to think the best conjurer in such a case would be an able-bodied cat," he said, with a provoking chuckle.

"But let us hear your own adventure," I said tartly.

At this challenge he looked uneasily round him. I had poked up a very unpleasant recollection.

"You shall hear it, Dick; I'll tell it to you," he said. "Begad, sir, I should feel quite queer, though, telling it *here*, though we are too strong a body for ghosts to meddle with just now."

Though he spoke this like a joke, I think it was serious calculation. Our Hebe was in a corner of the room, packing our cracked delf tea and dinner-services in a basket. She soon suspended operations, and with mouth and eyes wide open became an absorbed listener. Tom's experiences were told nearly in these words:—

"I saw it three times, Dick—three distinct times; and I am perfectly certain it meant me some infernal harm. I was, I say, in danger—in *extreme* danger; for, if nothing else had happened, my reason would most certainly have failed me, unless I had escaped so soon. Thank God. I *did* escape.

"The first night of this hateful disturbance, I was lying in the attitude of sleep, in that lumbering old bed. I hate to think of it. I was really wide awake, though I had put out my candle, and was lying as quietly as if I had been asleep; and although accidentally restless, my thoughts were running in a cheerful and agreeable channel.

"I think it must have been two o'clock at least when I thought I heard a sound in that—that odious dark recess at the far end of the bedroom. It was as if someone was drawing a piece of cord slowly along the floor, lifting it up, and dropping it softly down again in coils. I sate up once or twice in my bed, but could see nothing, so I concluded it must be mice in the wainscot. I felt no emotion graver than curiosity, and after a few minutes ceased to observe it.

"While lying in this state, strange to say; without at first a suspicion of anything supernatural, on a sudden I saw an old man, rather stout and square, in a sort of roan-red dressing-gown, and with a black cap on his head, moving stiffly and slowly in a diagonal direction, from the recess, across the floor of the bedroom, passing my bed at the foot, and entering the lumber-closet at the left. He had something under his arm; his head hung a litde at one side; and merciful God! when I saw his face."

Tom stopped for a while, and then said—

"That awful countenance, which living or dying I never can forget, disclosed what he was. Without turning to the right or left, he passed beside me, and entered the closet by the bed's head.

"While this fearful and indescribable type of death and guilt was passing, I felt that I had no more power to speak or stir than if I had been myself a corpse. For hours after it had disappeared, I was too terrified and weak to move. As soon as daylight came, I took courage, and examined the room, and especially the course which the frightful intruder had seemed to take, but there was not a vestige to indicate anybody's having passed there; no sign of any disturbing agency visible ambng the lumber that strewed the floor of the closet.

"I now began to recover a little. I was fagged and exhausted, and at last, overpowered by a feverish sleep. I came down late; and finding you out of spirits, on account of your dreams about the portrait, whose *original* I am now certain disclosed himself to me, I did not care to talk about the infernal vision. In fact, I was trying to persuade myself that the whole thing was an illusion, and I did not like to revive in their intensity the hated impressions of the past night— or, to risk the constancy of my scepticism, by recounting the tale of my sufferings.

"It required some nerve, I can tell you, to go to my haunted chamber next night, and lie down quietly in the same bed," continued Tom. "I did so with a degree of trepidation, which, I am not ashamed to say, a very little matter would have sufficed to stimulate to downright panic. This night, however, passed off quietly enough, as also the next; and so too did two or three more. I grew more confident, and began to fancy that I believed in the theories of spectral illusions, with which I had at first vainly tried to impose upon my convictions.

"The apparition had been, indeed, altogether anomalous. It had crossed the room without any recognition of my presence: I had not disturbed *it*, and *it* had no mission to *me*. What, then, was the imaginable use of its crossing the room in a visible shape at all? Of course it might have *been* in the closet instead of *going* there, as easily as it introduced itself into the recess without entering the chamber in a shape discernible by the senses. Besides, how the deuce *had* I seen it? It was a dark night; I had no candle; there was no fire; and yet I saw it as distinctly, in colouring and outline, as ever I beheld human form! A cataleptic dream would explain it all; and I was determined that a dream it should be.

"One of the most remarkable phenomena connected with the practice of mendacity is the vast number of deliberate lies we tell ourselves, whom, of all persons, we can least expect to deceive. In all this, I need hardly tell you, Dick, I was simply lying to myself, and did not believe one word of the wretched humbug. Yet I went on, as men will do, like persevering charlatans and impostors, who tire people into credulity by the mere force of reiteration; so I hoped to win myself over at last to a comfortable scepticism about the ghost.

"He had not appeared a second time—that certainly was a comfort; and what, after all, did I care for him, and his queer old toggery and strange looks? Not a fig! I was nothing the worse for having seen him, and a good story the better. So I tumbled into bed, put out my candle, and, cheered by a loud drunken quarrel in the back lane, went fast asleep.

"From this deep slumber I awoke with a start. I knew I had had a horrible dream; but what it was I could not remember. My heart was thumping furiously; I felt bewildered and feverish; I sate up in the bed and looked about the room. A broad flood of moonlight came in through the curtainless window; everything was as I had last seen it; and though the domestic squabble in the back lane was, unhappily for me, allayed, I yet could hear a pleasant fellow singing, on his way home, the then popular comic ditty called, 'Murphy Delany.' Taking advantage of this diversion I lay down again, with my face towards the fireplace, and closing my eyes, did my best to think of nothing else but the song, which was every moment growing fainter in the distance:—

' *'Twas Murphy Delany, so funny and frisky,*
Stept into a shebeen shop to get his skin full;
He reeled out again pretty well lined with whiskey,
As fresh as a shamrock, as blind as a bull.'

"The singer, whose condition I dare say resembled that of his hero, was soon too far off to regale my ears any more; and as his music died away, I myself sank into a doze, neither sound nor refreshing. Somehow the song had got into my head, and I went meandering on through the adventures of my respectable fellow-countryman, who, on emerging from the 'shebeen shop,' fell into a river, from which he was fished up to be 'sat upon' by a coroner's jury, who having learned from a 'horse-doctor' that he was 'dead as a door-nail, so there was an end,' returned their verdict accordingly, just as he returned to his senses, when an angry altercation and a pitched battle between the body and the coroner winds up the lay with due spirit and pleasantry.

"Through this ballad I continued with a weary monotony to plod, down to the very last line, and then *da capo*, and so on, in my uncomfortable half-sleep, for how long, I can't conjecture. I found myself at last, however, muttering, '*dead* as a door-nail, so there was an end'; and something like another voice within me, seemed to say, very faintly, but sharply, 'dead! dead! *dead*! and may the Lord have mercy on your soul!" and instantaneously I was wide awake, and staring right before me from the pillow.

"Now—will you believe it, Dick?—I saw the same accursed figure standing full front, and gazing at me with its stony and fiendish countenance, not two yards from the bedside."

Tom stopped here, and wiped the perspiration from his face. I felt very queer. The girl was as pale as Tom; and, assembled as we were in the very scene of these adventures, we were all, I dare say, equally grateful for the clear daylight and the resuming bustle out of doors.

"For about three seconds only I saw it plainly; then it grew indistinct; but, for a long time, there was something like a column of dark vapour where it had been standing between me and the wall; and I felt sure that he was still there. After a good while, this appearance went too. I took my clothes downstairs to the hall, and dressed there, with the door half open; then went out into the street, and walked about the town till morning, when I came back, in a miserable state of nervousness and exhaustion. I was such a fool, Dick, as to be ashamed to tell you how I came to be so upset. I thought you would laugh at me; especially as I had always talked philosophy, and treated *your* ghosts with contempt. I concluded you would give me no quarter; and so kept my tale of horror to myself.

"Now, Dick, you will hardly believe me, when I assure you, that for many nights after this last experience, I did not go to my room at all. I used to sit up for a while in the drawing-room after you had gone up to your bed; and then steal down softly to the hall-door, let myself out, and sit in the 'Robin Hood' tavern until the last guest went off; and then I got through the night like a sentry, pacing the streets till morning.

"For more than a week I never slept in bed. I sometimes had a snooze on a form in the 'Robin Hood,' and sometimes a nap in a chair during the day; but regular sleep I had absolutely none.

"I was quite resolved that we should get into another house; but I could not bring myself to tell you the reason, and I somehow put it off from day to day, although my life was, during every hour of this procrastination, rendered as miserable as that of a felon with the constables on his track. I was growing absolutely ill from this wretched mode of life.

"One afternoon I determined to enjoy an hour's sleep upon your bed. I hated mine; so that I had never, except in a stealthy visit every day to unmake it, lest Martha should discover the secret of my nightly absence, entered the ill-omened chamber.

"As ill-luck would have it, you had locked your bedroom,

and taken away the key. I went into my own to unsettle the bedclothes, as usual, and give the bed the appearance of having been slept in. Now, a variety of circumstances concurred to bring about the dreadful scene through which I was that night to pass. In the first place, I was literally overpowered with fatigue, and longing for sleep; in the next place, the effect of this extreme exhaustion upon my nerves resembled that of a narcotic, and rendered me less susceptible than, perhaps I should in any other condition have been, of the exciting fears which had become habitual to me. Then again, a little bit of the window was open, a pleasant freshness pervaded the room, and, to crown all, the cheerful sun of day was making the room quite pleasant. What was to prevent my enjoying an hour's nap *here*? The whole air was resonant with the cheerful hum of life, and the broad matter-of-fact light of day filled every corner of the room.

"I yielded—stifling my qualms—to the almost overpowering temptation; and merely throwing off my coat, and loosening my cravat, I lay down, limiting myself to *half-an-hour's* doze in the unwonted enjoyment of a feather bed, a coverlet, and a bolster.

"It was horribly insidious; and the demon, no doubt, marked my infatuated preparations. Dolt that I was, I fancied, with mind and body worn out for want of sleep, and an arrear of a full week's rest to my credit, that such measure as *half*-an-hour's sleep, in such a situation, was possible. My sleep was death-like, long, and dreamless.

"Without a start or fearful sensation of any kind, I waked gendy, but completely. It was, as you have good reason to remember, long past midnight—I believe, about two o'clock. When sleep has been deep and long enough to satisfy nature thoroughly, one often wakens in this way, suddenly, tranquilly, and completely.

"There was a figure seated in that lumbering, old sofa-chair, near the fireplace. Its back was rather towards me, but I could not be mistaken; it turned slowly round, and, merciful heavens! there was the stony face, with its infernal lineaments of malignity and despair, gloating on me. There was now no doubt as to its consciousness of my presence, and the hellish malice with which it was animated, for it arose, and drew close to the bedside. There was a rope about its neck, and the other end, coiled up, it held stiffly in its hand.

"My good angel nerved me for this horrible crisis. I remained for some seconds transfixed by the gaze of this tremendous phantom. He came close to the bed, and appeared on the point of mounting upon it. The next instant I was upon the floor at the far side, and in a moment more was, I don't know how, upon the lobby.

"But the spell was not yet broken; the valley of the shadow of death was not yet traversed. The abhorred phantom was before me there; it was standing near the banisters, stooping a little, and with one end of the rope round its own neck, was poising a noose at the other, as if to throw over mine; and while engaged in this baleful pantomime, it wore a smile so sensual, so unspeakably dreadful, that my senses were nearly overpowered. I saw and remember nothing more, until I found myself in your room.

"I had a wonderful escape, Dick—there is no disputing *that*—an escape for which, while I live, I shall bless the mercy of heaven. No one can conceive or imagine what it is for flesh and blood to stand in the presence of such a thing, but one who has had the terrific experience. Dick, Dick, a shadow has passed over me—a chill has crossed my blood and marrow, and I will never be the same again—never, Dick—never!"

Our handmaid, a mature girl of two-and-fifty, as I have said, stayed her hand, as Tom's story proceeded, and by little and little drew near to us, with open mouth, and her brows contracted over her little, beady black eyes, till stealing a glance over her shoulder now and then, she established herself close behind us. During the relation, she had made various earnest comments, in an undertone; but these and her ejaculations, for the sake of brevity and simplicity, I have omitted in my narration.

"It's often I heard tell of it," she now said, "but I never believed it rightly till now—though, indeed, why should not I? Does not my mother, down there in the lane, know quare stories, God bless us, beyant telling about it? But you ought not to have slept in the back bedroom. She was loath to let me be going in and out of that room even in the day time, let alone for any Christian to spend the night in it; for sure she says it was his own bedroom."

"*Whose* own bedroom?" we asked, in a breath.

"Why, *his*—the ould Judge's—Judge Horrock's, to be sure, God rest his sowl"; and she looked fearfully round.

"Amen!" I muttered. "But did he die there?"

"Die there! No, not quite *there*" she said. "Shure, was not it over the banisters he hung himself, the ould sinner, God be merciful to us all? and was not it in the alcove they found the handles of the skipping-rope cut off, and the knife where he was settling the cord, God bless us, to hang himself with? It was his housekeeper's daughter owned the rope, my mother often told me, and the child never throve after, and used to be starting up out of her sleep, and screeching in the night time, wid dhrames and frights that cum an her; and they said how it was the speerit of the ould Judge that was tormentin' her; and she used to be roaring and yelling out to hould back the big ould fellow with the crooked neck; and then she'd screech 'Oh, the master! the master! he's stampin' at me, and beckoning to me! Mother, darling, don't let me go!' And so the poor crathure died at last, and the docthers said it was wather on the brain, for it was all they could say."

"How long ago was all this?" I asked.

"Oh, then, how would I know?" she answered. "But it must be a wondherful long time ago, for the housekeeper was an ould woman, with a pipe in her mouth, and not a tooth left, and better nor eighty years ould when my mother was first married; and they said she was a rale buxom, fine-dressed woman when the ould Judge come to his end; an', indeed, my mother's not far from eighty years ould herself this day; and what made it worse for the unnatural ould villain, God rest his soul, to frighten the little girl out of the world the way he did, was what was mostly thought and believed by everyone. My mother says how the poor little crathure was his own child; for he was by all accounts an ould villain every way, an' the hangin'est judge that ever was known in Ireland's ground."

"From what you said about the danger of sleeping in that bedroom," said I, "I suppose there were stories about the ghost having appeared there to others."

"Well, there *was* things said—quare things, surely," she answered, as it seemed, with some reluctance. "And why would not there? Sure was it not up in that same room he slept for more than twenty years? and was it not in the *alcove* he got the rope ready that done his own business at last, the way he done many a betther man's in his lifetime?—and was not the body lying in the same bed after death, and put in the coffin there, too, and carried out to his grave from it in Pether's churchyard, after the coroner was done? But there was quare stories—my mother has them all—about how one Nicholas Spaight got into trouble on the head of it."

"And what did they say of this Nicholas Spaight?" I asked.

"Oh, for that matther, it's soon told," she answered.

And she certainly did relate a very strange story, which so piqued my curiosity, that I took occasion to visit the ancient lady, her mother, from whom I learned many very curious particulars. Indeed, I am tempted to tell the tale, but my fingers are weary, and I must defer it. But if you wish to hear it another time, I shall do my best.

When we had heard the strange tale I have *not* told you, we put one or two further questions to her about the alleged spectral visitations, to which the house had, ever since the death of the wicked old Judge, been subjected.

"No one ever had luck in it," she told us. "There was always cross accidents, sudden deaths, and short times in it. The first that tuck it was a family—I forget their name—but at any rate there was two young ladies and their papa.

He was about sixty, and a stout healthy gentleman as you'd wish to see at that age. Well, he slept in that unlucky back bedroom; and, God between us an' harm! sure enough he was found dead one morning, half out of the bed, with his head as black as a sloe, and swelled like a puddin', hanging down near the floor. It was a fit, they said. He was as dead as a mackerel, and so *he* could not say what it was; but the ould people was all sure that it was nothing at all but the ould Judge, God bless us! that frightened him out of his senses and his life together.

"Some time after there was a rich old maiden lady took the house. I don't know which room *she* slept in, but she lived alone; and at any rate, one morning, the servants going down early to their work, found her sitting on the passage-stairs, shivering and talkin' to herself, quite mad; and never a word more could any of *them* or her friends get from her ever afterwards but, 'Don't ask me to go, for I promised to wait for him.' They never made out from her who it was she meant by *him*, but of course those that knew all about the ould house were at no loss for the meaning of all that happened to her.

"Then afterwards, when the house was let out in lodgings, there was Micky Byrne that took the same room, with his wife and three little children; and sure I heard Mrs. Byrne myself telling how the children used to be lifted up in the bed at night, she could not see by what mains; and how they were starting and screeching every hour, just all as one as the housekeeper's little girl that died, till at last one night poor Micky had a dhrop in him, the way he used now and again; and what do you think in the middle of the night he thought he heard a noise on the stairs, and being in liquor, nothing less id do him but out he must go himself to see what was wrong. Well, after that, all she ever heard of him was himself sayin', 'Oh, God!' and a tumble that shook the very house; and there, sure enough, he was lying on the lower stairs, under the lobby, with his neck smashed double undher him, where he was flung over the banisters."

Then the handmaiden added—

"I'll go down to the lane, and send up Joe Gawey to pack up the rest of the taythings, and bring all the things across to your new lodgings."

And so we all sallied out together, each of us breathing more freely, I have no doubt, as we crossed that ill-omened threshold for the last time.

Now, I may add thus much, in compliance with the immemorial usage of the realm of fiction, which sees the hero not only through his adventures, but fairly out of the world. You must have perceived that what the flesh, blood, and bone hero of romance proper is to the regular compounder of fiction, this old house of brick, wood, and mortar is to the humble recorder of this true tale. I, therefore, relate, as in duty bound, the catastrophe which ultimately befell it, which was simply this—that about two years subsequently to my story it was taken by a quack doctor, who called himself Baron Duhlstoerf, and filled the parlour windows with bottles of indescribable horrors preserved in brandy, and the newspapers with the usual grandiloquent and mendacious advertisements. This gentleman among his virtues did not reckon sobriety, and one night, being overcome with much wine, he set fire to his bed curtains, partially burned himself, and totally consumed the house. It was afterwards rebuilt, and for a time an undertaker established himself in the premises.

I have now told you my own and Tom's adventures, together with some valuable collateral particulars; and having acquitted myself of my engagement, I wish you a very good night, and pleasant dreams.

ENCOUNTER AT NIGHT

Mary Frances McHugh

Dublin was growing deserted; only an odd car slid by in the dark, rainy night, for the second of its passing throwing a dazzle on the shiny pavements and lighting up the shuttered shops. Figures would pass, hurrying by with hunched shoulders—but less and less frequently.

Tom Donovan and his three friends scarcely felt the rain. They were hot and happy and bemused. All that each of them wanted was somehow to continue talking and drinking and smoking in genial company . . . But Jim, the red-haired barman at Flynn's, had gradually edged them out into the night, and bolted the doors against them. There was nothing for it but to go home.

'Take care of yourself, Joe!'

'Well, goodnight, boys!'

'Take care—see you tomorrow.'

The milk of human kindness flowed in them, and they patted one another's backs affectionately again and again before each went his separate way. Donovan, the shiftless poet, was left standing on the pavement, last and lonely. Slowly there faded from his face its smile of convivial bliss, and into his sobering mind crept back those thoughts which now, with the fleeting years, possessed him more and more in his solitary moments.

Wretched, killing thoughts. No, not thoughts—not thoughts, but feelings—or one feeling only, corroding unhappiness. A sense that life was vain and empty, with comfort nowhere—not even in drinking, in friendship, or in love. If even he knew friendship or love! A certainty that never, during all his existence, even when he had been young and gay and roistering, had he known ease: always a shadow had been lurking at his elbow. And it whispered to him that he was a fool to go on with the sham from day to day, that there was only one solution to everything: a knife or a rope for his throat.

Cruel memories came thronging. He saw a miserable, beaten peasant child: himself. All that child had really known was suffering, though the man had made sweet lilting songs of a boy, barefooted, in the West, birds'-nesting or tickling for trout in a mountain stream. The boy had been there, the sun, the stream, the idyllic sky, the irrational light-heartedness of childhood. These were the stuff of his verse—but not the harsh home, the pain and puzzled grief, the cold and hunger which had been more true and near. These things had made him!—they were with him even now.

Later, there was the man. A poet he was now, praised and wondered at for the clear innocency of his songs, toys fashioned for the cultured mind by a queer bohemian fellow. That he was so different from his poetry merely gave it zest. He knew this, and cultivated his oddity; and it was partly to curry favour with his admirers that he drank and sang his way through Europe without a word of any language but his own. Here, standing on a Dublin pavement in the night, he recalled the troubadour adventure and shivered—not because the steely rain was stinging his face and sending cold arrows through his clothing. No; but because from those wanderings from which he had so triumphantly returned he could now remember only a haunting horror. He evoked without willing it a night in Russia, when he lay in a country tavern with his familiar spirit beside him. There, in a big common room, several poor travellers slept about the stove. The air was humid with their breath and the odorous damp of their clothing, and the windows were sealed to blindness by the snow outside. In the yard there suddenly arose the commotion of a sledge being unharnessed; a bulky figure stepped into the room and looked stealthily around at the sleepers and fixedly at him, Donovan, before flinging itself likewise down in a corner. Donovan through half-closed eyes saw the stranger's Mongolian face, and as though he were a child it smote him with its mystery of a locked mind, of a race other than and alien to his own. There was no reason for his sudden panic of fear, or for the anguish of loneliness which overcame him then. It was simply part of the encompassing oppression of the world to his soul, driving him whither he knew not.

He tossed his head, heedless of the rain, appealing to the sky above him to protect and save. There must be rest somewhere, a cooling of this fever: why should he, more than other men, be so tormented? Why could he not be like little Terry Shaughnessy, caring nothing for anyone, whether drunk or sober, in funds or out of them? Now, there was an idea! Why go back, in this mood and in this weather, to his cold room and unwelcoming bed, when Terry would be glad enough for him to drop in for a smoke and a talk? He'd be there, sure enough, in his attic in Eustace Street. He wouldn't be in bed. Who ever heard of little Terry being in bed? He'd have a warm fire, and maybe a taste of something—'one for the worms,' as he called it . . . Donovan turned towards Eustace Street.

He trotted along mechanically, now thinking cheerfully of himself and Terry. They were the only bachelors among the boys—and taking it all in all, he'd swear they were as well off like that. He thought of Ned Buckley's wife, and grinned to himself. A nice exhibition she made of the poor man, running to his newspaper office or writing to the editor when she wanted money. Ned was a good sort—but what kind of man was he to put up with that? Now, if any woman tried to manage *him*—! Or Terry: he'd swear Terry would know how to deal with her, too. Keep a firm hand. That was it.

Yet, maybe—Terry as well as himself—in their hearts they'd like to have a home, and a woman waiting for them, and children. Maybe they'd die in the workhouse, no one caring enough for them to follow them to the grave . . . At these sad thoughts Donovan's mouth turned down again behind his coat collar, and he felt nearly dismal enough to cry. But resolutely he clung to the advantages of his state. He was his own master, anyway. He could drop in on Terry like this, tonight, and Terry be welcome to drop in on him, any hour he liked.

The rain beat on his face, stood in tears on his eyelashes till the street lamps carried a halo, each of them. Then he blinked and shook his head, and the long, deserted street shone straight before him again. A clock struck twelve. Ah, here was Terry's door. God, it was good to get in out of the rain!

The door stood ajar. That saved ringing the bell. Probably someone had left it like that on purpose—goodness knew how many lived in the old rookery. Not a glimmer of light.

But Donovan felt his way to the banisters, gripped them, and mounted, cautiously counting the stairs.

Terry's door was opposite the fourth turn. Two . . . three . . . The next one . . . *Mother of God, what was that?*

Someone, coming out of the darkness, had struck him softly. A blow of a doubled-up fist in the face. Like a joke, by the Lord! But where had the fellow got to?

'Who's that?' called out Donovan, his voice a little startled in the night. 'Who's there? What the blazes are you doing.?'

There was no answer. Donovan crouched a moment in the darkness, very still, then changed his walking-stick to the other hand. But he must have been flustered, for his fingers didn't catch on it, and down it went clattering against the uncarpeted stairs, stopping once, clattering again, staying finally where it was. He stopped and groped, but thought better of going back for it. He stared about him and in the blackness thought he saw a solider patch, a man facing him a couple of steps up. That was the man who had struck him. But why on earth didn't he say something?

'Who's there?' he shouted again. 'Speak up, whoever you are!'

There was no answer, so he stepped forward boldly. But again someone pushed him—pushed him so plainly, as though with a playful gentleness, that he could feel the woollen jacket of the shoulder thrust against him. As in indignant alarm he tried to grasp it, it silently eluded him, moving soundlessly, eerily, out of reach.

Donovan's blood crept in his veins, and his heart seemed to lunge downwards in his body. Suddenly he wished he felt steadier, that he hadn't had so many drinks. Then he thought instinctively how another good stiff whisky would hearten him—yes, give him fire to tell this sly fellow, whoever the hell he was, what he thought of him.

He paused and gasped, listening with all his ears. Not a sound could he catch; and swiftly changing mood, convinced that it was only some silly trick being played on him, he became wildly angry.

'Come on!' he shouted, his excited voice falling back to the cadence of his native West. 'Come on, you puppy! Come on, you coward you, if you're a man at all, and I'll wrastle you in the Connemara fashion!'

He bent down over his right knee in an attitude of defence. 'I'll fight you! I'll wrastle you!' he repeated belligerently.

For a few seconds he held up his fists, awaiting his assailant. But the latter did not move. Then, like a bull, Donovan made to rush up the stairs. *Ah!*—With a soft thud he struck his head into the stomach of the lurking enemy. The invisible man, silent and unshocked, moved stealthily away.

But Donovan followed him, and as he did so was surprised

to find the other coming towards him. He flung away caution and grasped his man about the body. Something rigid but yielding, human yet cold, lay unprotestingly within his arms. He released it and stepped back, weak and shuddering.

It swung—it hung . . . Ah, God!

Donovan recoiled, as sober as at morning. For a full minute he waited where he stood, overwhelmed with a nameless dread. Then he struck a match and, peering up, saw above him the blackened face of little Terry Shaughnessy, hanging from his attic banisters . . .

FOOTSTEPS IN THE LOBBY

Joseph Sheridan Le Fanu

I went to my room early that night, but I was too miserable to sleep. At about twelve o'clock, feeling very nervous, I determined to call my cousin Emily, who slept in the next room, which communicated with mine by a second door. By this private entrance I found my way into her chamber, and without difficulty persuaded her to return to my room and sleep with me. We accordingly lay down together—she undressed, and I with my clothes on—for I was every moment walking up and down the room, and felt too nervous and miserable to think of rest or comfort. Emily was soon fast asleep, and I lay awake, fervently longing for the first pale gleam of morning, reckoning every stroke of the old clock with an impatience which made every hour appear like six.

It must have been about one o'clock when I thought I heard a slight noise at the partition door between Emily's room and mine, as if caused by somebody's turning the key in the lock. I held my breath, and the same sound was repeated at the second door of my room—that which opened upon the lobby—the sound was here distinctly caused by the revolution of the bolt in the lock, and it was followed by a slight pressure upon the door itself, as if to ascertain the security of the lock. The person, whoever it might be, was probably satisfied, for I heard the old boards of the lobby creak and strain, as if under the weight of somebody moving cautiously over them.

My sense of hearing became unnaturally, almost painfully acute. I suppose the imagination added distinctness to sounds vague in themselves. I thought that I could actually hear the breathing of the person who was slowly returning down the lobby; at the head of the staircase there appeared to occur a pause; and I could distinctly hear two or three sentences hastily whispered; the steps then descended the stairs with apparently less caution. I now ventured to walk quickly and lightly to the lobby door, and attempted to open it; but it was indeed fast locked upon the outside, as was also the other. I now felt that the dreadful hour was come; but one desperate expedient remained—it was to awaken Emily, and by our united strength, to attempt to force the partition door, which was slighter than the other, and through this to pass to the lower part of the house, whence it might be possible to escape to the grounds, and forth to the village.

I returned to the bedside, and shook Emily, but in vain; nothing that I could do availed to produce from her more than a few incoherent words—it was a death-like sleep. She had certainly drunk of some narcotic, as had I probably also, in spite of all the caution with which I had examined everything presented to us to eat or drink. I now attempted, with as little noise as possible, to force first one door, then the other—but all in vain. I believe no strength could have effected my object, for both doors opened inwards. I therefore collected whatever movables I could carry thither, and piled them against the doors, so as to assist me in whatever attempts I should make to resist the entrance of those without. I then returned to the bed and endeavoured again, but fruitlessly, to awaken my cousin. It was not sleep, it was torpor, lethargy, death. I knelt down and prayed with an agony of earnestness; and then seating myself upon the bed, I awaited my fate with a kind of terrible tranquillity.

I heard a faint clanking sound from the narrow court below, as if caused by the scraping of some iron instrument against stones or rubbish. I at first determined not to disturb the calmness which I now felt, by uselessly watching the proceedings of those who sought my life; but as the sounds continued, the horrible curiosity which I felt overcame every other emotion, and I determined, at all hazards, to gratify it.

I therefore crawled upon my knees to the window, so as to let the smallest portion of my head appear above the sill.

The moon was shining with an uncertain radiance upon the antique grey buildings, and obliquely upon the narrow court beneath, one side of which was therefore clearly illuminated, while the other was lost in obscurity, the sharp outlines of the old gables, with their nodding clusters of ivy, being at first alone visible. Whoever or whatever occasioned the noise which had excited my curiosity, was concealed under the shadow of the dark side of the quadrangle. I placed my hand over my eyes to shade them from the moonlight, which was so bright as to be almost dazzling, and, peering into the darkness, I first dimly, but afterwards gradually, almost with full distinctness, beheld the form of a man engaged in digging what appeared to be a rude hole close under the wall. Some implements, probably a shovel and pickaxe, lay beside him, and to these he every now and then applied himself as the nature of the ground required. He pursued his task rapidly, and with as little noise as possible.

'So,' thought I, as shovelful after shovelful the dislodged rubbish mounted into a heap, 'they are digging the grave in which, before two hours pass, I must lie, a cold, mangled corpse. I am *theirs*—I cannot escape.' I felt as if my reason was leaving me. I started to my feet, and in mere despair I applied myself again to each of the two doors alternately.

I strained every nerve and sinew, but I might as well have attempted, with my single strength, to force the building itself from its foundation. I threw myself madly upon the ground, and clasped my hands over my eyes as if to shut out the horrible images which crowded upon me.

The paroxysm passed away. I prayed once more with the bitter, agonised fervour of one who feels that the hour of death is present and inevitable. When I arose I went once more to the window and looked out, just in time to see a shadowy figure glide stealthily along the wall. The task was finished. The catastrophe of the tragedy must soon be accomplished. I determined now to defend my life to the last; and that I might be able to do so with some effect, I searched the room for something which might serve as a weapon; but either through accident, or from an anticipation of such a possibility, everything which might have been made available for such a purpose had been carefully removed. I must thus die tamely and without an effort to defend myself.

A thought suddenly struck me—might it not be possible to escape through the door, which the assassin must open in order to enter the room? I resolved to make the attempt. I felt assured that the door through which ingress to the room would be effected was that which opened upon the lobby. It was the more direct way, besides being, for obvious reasons, less liable to interruption than the other. I resolved then to place myself behind a projection of the wall, whose shadow would serve fully to conceal me, and when the door should be opened, and before they should have discovered the identity of the occupant of the bed, to creep noiselessly from the room, and then to trust to Providence for escape. In order to facilitate this scene, I removed all the lumber which I had heaped against the door; and I had nearly completed my arrangements, when I perceived the room suddenly darkened by the close approach of some shadowy object to the window. On turning my eyes in that direction, I observed at the top of the casement, as if suspended from above, first the feet, then the legs, then the body, and at length the whole figure of a man present itself.

It was Edward T——n. He appeared to be guiding his descent so as to bring his feet upon the centre of the stone block which occupied the lower part of the window; and having secured his footing upon this, he kneeled down and began to gaze into the room. As the moon was gleaming into the chamber, and the bed curtains were drawn, he was able to distinguish the bed itself and its contents. He appeared satisfied with his scrutiny, for he looked up and made a sign with his hand, upon which the rope by which his descent had been effected was slackened from above, and he proceeded to disengage it from his waist: this accomplished, he applied his hands to the window-frame, which must have been ingeniously contrived for the purpose, for with apparently no resistance the whole frame, containing casement and all, slipped from its position in the wall, and was by him lowered into the room. The cold night waved the bed-curtains, and he paused for a moment—all was still again—and he stepped in upon the floor of the room. He held in his hand what appeared to be a steel instrument, shaped something like a hammer, but larger and sharper at the extremities. This he held rather behind him, while, with three long *tip-toe* strides, he brought himself to the bedside.

I felt that the discovery must now be made, and held my breath in momentary expectation of the execration in which he would vent his surprise and disappointment. I closed my eyes—there was a pause—but it was a short one. I heard two dull blows, given in rapid succession: a quivering sigh, and the long-drawn, heavy breathing of the sleeper was for ever suspended. I unclosed my eyes, and saw the murderer fling the quilt across the head of his victim: he then, with the instrument of death still in his hand, proceeded to the lobby door, upon which he tapped sharply twice or thrice—a quick step was then heard approaching, and a voice whispered something from without—Edward answered, with a kind of chuckle, 'Her ladyship is past complaining; unlock the door, in the devil's name, unless you're afraid to come in, and help me to lift the body out of the window.' The key was turned in the lock—the door opened—and my uncle entered the room.

I have told you already that I had placed myself under the shade of a projection of the wall, close to the door. I had instinctively shrunk down cowering towards the ground on the entrance of Edward through the window. When my uncle entered the room, he and his son both stood so very close to me that his hand was every moment upon the point of touching my face. I held my breath, and remained motionless as death.

'You had no interruption from the next room?' said my uncle.

'No,' was the brief reply.

'Secure the jewels, Ned; the French harpy must not lay her claws upon them. You've a steady hand, by G—; not much blood—eh?'

'Not twenty drops,' replied his son, 'and those on the quilt.'

'I'm glad it's over,' whispered my uncle again; 'we must lift the—the *thing* through the window, and lay the rubbish over it.'

They then turned to the bedside, and, winding the bed-clothes round the body, carried it between them slowly to the window, and, exchanging a few brief words with someone below, they shoved it over the window sill, and I heard it fall heavily on the ground underneath.

'I'll take the jewels,' said my uncle; 'there are two caskets in the lower drawer.'

He proceeded, with an accuracy which, had I been more at ease, would have furnished me with matter of astonishment, to lay his hand upon the very spot where my jewels lay; and having possessed himself of them, he called to his son—

'Is the rope made fast above?'

'I'm not a fool—to be sure it is,' replied he.

They then lowered themselves from the window. I now rose lightly and cautiously, scarcely daring to breathe, from my place of concealment, and was creeping towards the door, when I heard my cousin's voice, in a sharp whisper, exclaim, 'Scramble up again; G—d d—n you, you've forgot to lock the door;' and I perceived, by the straining of the rope which hung from above, that the mandate was instantly obeyed.

Not a second was to be lost. I passed through the door, which was only closed, and moved as rapidly as I could, consistently with stillness, along the lobby. Before I had gone many yards I heard the door through which I had just passed double locked on the inside. I glided down the stairs in terror, lest, at every corner, I should meet the murderer or one of his accomplices. I reached the hall, and listened for a moment to ascertain whether all was silent around; no sound was audible; the parlour windows opened on the park, and through one of them I might, I thought, easily effect my escape. Accordingly, I hastily entered; but, to my consternation, a candle was burning in the room, and by its light I saw a figure seated at the dinner-table, upon which lay glasses, bottles, and the other accompaniments of a drinking party.

There was no other means of escape, so I advanced with a firm step and collected mind to the window. I noiselessly withdrew the bars and unclosed the shutters—I pushed open the casement, and, without waiting to look behind me, I ran with my utmost speed, scarcely feeling the ground under me, down the avenue, taking care to keep upon the grass which bordered it. I did not for a moment slack my speed, and I had now gained the centre point between the park gate and the mansion-house—here the avenue made a wider circuit, and in order to avoid delay, I directed my way across the smooth sward round which the pathway wound, intending, at the opposite side of the flat, at a point which I distinguished by a group of old birch trees, to enter again upon the beaten track, which was from thence tolerably direct to the gate.

I had, with my utmost speed, got about halfway across this broad flat when the rapid treading of a horse's hoofs struck upon my ear. My heart swelled in my bosom, as though I would smother. The clattering of galloping hoofs approached—I was pursued—they were now upon the sward on which I was running—there was not a bush or a bramble to shelter me—and, as if to render escape altogether desperate, the moon, which had hitherto been obscured, at this moment shone forth with a broad clear light, which made every object distinctly visible. The sounds were now close behind me. I felt my knees bending under me, with the sensation which torments one in dreams. I reeled—I stumbled—I fell—and at the same instant the cause of my alarm wheeled past me at full gallop. It was one of the young fillies which pastured loose about the park, whose frolics had thus all but maddened me with terror.

I scrambled to my feet, and rushed on with weak but rapid steps, my sportive companion still galloping round and round me with many a frisk and fling, until, at length, more dead than alive, I reached the avenue gate and crossed the stile, I scarce knew how. I ran through the village, in which all was silent as the grave, until my progress was arrested by the hoarse voice of a sentinel, who cried, 'Who goes there?' I felt that I was now safe. I turned in the direction of the voice, and fell fainting at the soldier's feet.

When I came to myself I was sitting in a miserable hovel, surrounded by strange faces, all bespeaking curiosity and compassion. Many soldiers were in it also; indeed, as I afterwards found, it was employed as a guard-room by a detachment of troops quartered for that night in the town. In a few words I informed their officer of the circumstances which had occurred, describing also the appearance of the persons engaged in the murder; and he, without loss of time, proceeded to the mansion-house of Carrickleigh, taking with him a number of his men. But the villains had discovered their mistake, and had effected their escape, before the arrival of the military.

Deep and fervent as must always be my gratitude to Heaven for my deliverance, effected by a chain of providential occurrences, the failing of a single link of which must have insured my destruction, I was long before I could look back upon it with other feelings than those of bitterness, almost of agony. My cousin, the only being that had ever really loved me, my nearest dearest friend, ever ready to sympathise, to counsel, and to assist—the gayest, the gentlest, the warmest heart—the only creature on earth that cared for me—*her* life had been the price of my deliverance; and I then uttered the wish—which no event of my long and sorrowful life has taught me to recall—that she had been spared, and that in her stead *I* were mouldering in the grave forgotten and at rest.

IRISH WITCH TALES

Lady Wilde

THE LADY WITCH

About a hundred years ago there lived a woman in Joyce's Country, of whom all the neighbours were afraid, for she had always plenty of money, though no one knew how she came by it; and the best of eating and drinking went on at her house, chiefly at night—meat and fowls and Spanish wines in plenty for all comers. And when people asked how it all came, she laughed and said, "I have paid for it," but would tell them no more.

So the word went through the country that she had sold herself to the Evil One, and could have everything she wanted by merely wishing and willing, and because of her riches they called her "The Lady Witch."

She never went out but at night, and then always with a bridle and whip in her hand; and the sound of a horse galloping was heard often far on in the night along the roads near her house.

Then a strange story was whispered about, that if a young man drank of her Spanish wines at supper and afterwards fell asleep, she would throw the bridle over him and change him to a horse, and ride him all over the country, and whatever she touched with her whip became hers. Fowls, or butter, or wine, or the new-made cakes—she had but to wish and will and they were carried by spirit hands to her house, and laid in her larder. Then when the ride was done, and she had gathered enough through the country of all she wanted, she took the bridle off the young man, and he came back to his own shape and fell asleep; and when he awoke he had no knowledge of all that had happened, and the Lady Witch bade him come again and drink of her Spanish wines as often as it pleased him.

Now there was a fine brave young fellow in the neighbourhood, and he determined to make out the truth of the story. So he often went back and forwards, and made friends with the Lady Witch, and sat down to talk to her, but always on the watch. And she took a great fancy to him and told him he must come to supper some night, and she would give him the best of everything, and he must taste her Spanish wine.

So she named the night, and he went gladly, for he was filled with curiosity. And when he arrived there was a beautiful supper laid, and plenty of wine to drink; and he ate and drank, but was cautious about the wine, and spilled it on the ground from his glass when her head was turned away. Then he pretended to be very sleepy, and she said—

"My son, you are weary. Lie down there on the bench and sleep, for the night is far spent, and you are far from your home."

So he lay down as if he were quite dead with sleep, and closed his eyes, but watched her all the time.

Witches riding to the Sabbat. A superb engraving dated 1844.

*The popular Victorian idea of a witch. An illustration from
a collection of witchcraft stories published in 1856*

The interest in witchcraft during the Victorian era can be judged by the fact that one enterprising firm put out a whole series of specially-posed cards depicting various aspects of the subject. Here is one card showing a 'ducking' scene.

A harrowing illustration of a suspect under torture. See "The Amber Witch" by Lady Duff-Gordon.

And she came over in a little while and looked at him steadily, but he never stirred, only breathed the more heavily.

Then she went softly and took the bridle from the wall, and stole over to fling it over his head; but he started up, and, seizing the bridle threw it over the woman, who was immediately changed into a spanking grey mare. And he led her out and jumped on her back and rode away as fast as the wind till he came to the forge.

"Ho, smith," he cried, "rise up and shoe my mare, for she is weary after the journey."

And the smith got up and did his work as he was bid, well and strong. Then the young man mounted again, and rode back like the wind to the house of the Witch; and there he took off the bridle, and she immediately regained her own form, and sank down in a deep sleep.

But as the shoes had been put on at the forge without saying the proper form of words, they remained on her hands and feet, and no power on earth could remove them.

So she never rose from her bed again, and died not long after of grief and shame. And not one in the whole country would follow the coffin of the Lady Witch to the grave, and the bridle was burned with fire, and of all her riches nothing was left but a handful of ashes, and this was flung to the four points of earth and the four winds of heaven; so the enchantment was broken and the power of the Evil One ended.

THE DEMON CAT

There was a woman in Connemara, the wife of a fisherman; as he had always good luck, she had plenty of fish at all times stored away in the house ready for market. But, to her great annoyance, she found that a great cat used to come in at night and devour all the best and finest fish. So she kept a big stick by her, and determined to watch.

One day, as she and a woman were spinning together, the house suddenly became quite dark; and the door was burst open as if by the blast of the tempest, when in walked a huge black cat, who went straight up to the fire, then turned round and growled at them.

"Why, surely this is the devil," said a young girl, who was by, sorting fish.

"I'll teach you how to call me names," said the cat; and, jumping at her, he scratched her arm till the blood came. "There, now," he said, "you will be more civil another time when a gentleman comes to see you." And with that he walked over to the door and shut it close, to prevent any of them going out, for the poor young girl, while crying loudly from fright and pain, had made a desperate rush to get away.

Just then a man was going by, and hearing the cries, he pushed open the door and tried to get in; but the cat stood on the threshold, and would let no one pass. On this the man attacked him with his stick, and gave him a sound blow; the cat, however, was more than a match in the fight, for it flew at him and tore his face and hands so badly that the man at last took to his heels and ran away as fast as he could.

"Now, it's time for my dinner," said the cat, going up to examine the fish that was laid out on the tables. "I hope the fish is good today. Now, don't disturb me, nor make a fuss; I can help myself." With that he jumped up, and begun to devour all the best fish, while he growled at the woman.

"Away, out of this, you wicked beast," she cried, giving it a blow with the tongs that would have broken its back, only it was a devil; "out of this; no fish shall you have to-day."

But the cat only grinned at her, and went on tearing and spoiling and devouring the fish, evidently not a bit the worse for the blow. On this, both the women attacked it with sticks, and struck hard blows enough to kill it, on which the cat glared at them, and spit fire; then, making a leap, it tore their heads and arms till the blood came, and the frightened women rushed shrieking from the house.

But presently the mistress returned, carrying with her a bottle of holy water; and, looking in, she saw the cat still devouring the fish, and not minding. So she crept over quietly and threw holy water on it without a word. No sooner was this done than a dense black smoke filled the place, through which nothing was seen but the two red eyes of the cat, burning like coals of fire. Then the smoke gradually cleared away, and she saw the body of the creature burning slowly till it became shrivelled and black like a cinder, and finally disappeared. And from that time the fish remained untouched and safe from harm, for the power of the evil one was broken, and the demon cat was seen no more.

THE EVIL EYE

There is nothing more dreaded by the people, nor considered more deadly in its effects, than the Evil Eye.

There are several modes in which the Evil Eye can act, some much more deadly than others. If certain persons are met the first thing in the morning, you will be unlucky for the whole of that day in all you do. If the evil-eyed comes in to rest, and looks fixedly on anything, on cattle or on a child, there is doom in the glance; a fatality which cannot be evaded except by a powerful counter-charm. But if the evil-eyed mutters a verse over a sleeping child, that child will assuredly die, for the incantation is of the devil, and no charm has power to resist it or turn away the evil. Sometimes the process of bewitching is effected by looking fixedly at the object, through nine fingers; especially is the magic fatal if the victim is seated by the fire in the evening when the moon is full. Therefore, to avoid being suspected of having the Evil Eye, it is necessary at once, when looking at a child, to say "God bless it." And when passing a farmyard where the cows are collected for milking, to say, "The blessing of God be on you and on all your labours." If this form is omitted, the worst results may be apprehended, and the people would be filled with terror and alarm, unless a counter-charm were not instantly employed.

The singular malific influence of a glance has been felt by most persons in life; an influence that seems to paralyze intellect and speech, simply by the mere presence in the room of some one who is mystically antipathetic to our nature. For the soul is like a fine-toned harp that vibrates to the slightest external force or movement, and the presence and glance of some persons can radiate around us a divine joy, while others may kill the soul with a sneer or a frown. We call these subtle influences mysteries, but the early races believed them to be produced by spirits, good or evil, as they acted on the nerves or the intellect.

Some years ago an old woman was living in Kerry, and it was thought so unlucky to meet her in the morning, that all the girls used to go out after sunset to bring in water for the following day, that so they night avoid her evil glance; for whatever she looked on came to loss and grief.

There was a man, also, equally dreaded on account of the strange, fatal power of his glance; and so many accidents and misfortunes were traced to his presence that finally the neighbours insisted that he should wear a black patch over the Evil Eye, not to be removed unless by request; for learned gentlemen, curious in such things, sometimes came to him to ask for a proof of his power, and he would try it for a wager while drinking with his friends.

One day, near an old-ruin of a castle, he met a boy weeping

in great grief for his pet pigeon, which had got up to the very top of the ruin, and could not be coaxed down.

"What will you give me," asked the man, "if I bring it down for you?"

"I have nothing to give," said the boy, "but I will pray to God for you. Only get me back my pigeon, and I shall be happy."

Then the man took off the black patch and looked up steadfastly at the bird; when all of a sudden it fell to the ground and lay motionless as if stunned; but there was no harm done to it, and the boy took it up and went his way, rejoicing.

Some years ago a woman living in Kerry declared that she was "overlooked" by the Evil Eye. She had no pleasure in her life and no comfort, and she wasted away because of the fear that was on her, caused by the following singular circumstance:—

Every time that she happened to leave home alone, and that no one was within call, she was met by a woman totally unknown to her who, fixing her eyes on her in silence, with a terrible expression, cast her to the ground and proceeded to beat and pinch her till she was nearly senseless; after which her tormentor disappeared.

Having experienced this treatment several times, the poor woman finally abstained altogether from leaving the house, unless protected by a servant or companion; and this precaution she observed for several years, during which time she never was molested. So at last she began to believe that the spell was broken, and that her strange enemy had departed for ever.

In consequence she grew less careful about the usual precaution, and one day stepped down alone to a little stream that ran by the house to wash some clothes.

Stooping down over her work, she never thought of any danger, and began to sing as she used to do in the light-hearted days before the spell was on her, when suddenly a dark shadow fell across the water, and looking up, she beheld to her horror the strange woman on the opposite side of the little stream, with her terrible eyes intently fixed on her, as hard and still as if she were of stone.

Springing up with a scream of terror, she flung down her work, and ran towards the house; but soon she heard footsteps behind her, and in an instant she was seized, thrown down to the ground, and her tormentor began to beat her even worse than before, till she lost all consciousness; and in this state she was found by her husband, lying on her face and speechless. She was at once carried to the house, and all the care that affection and rural skill could bestow were lavished on her, but in vain. She, however, regained sufficient consciousness to tell them of the terrible encounter she had gone through, but died before the night had passed away.

It was believed that the power of fascination by the glance, which is not necessarily an evil power like the Evil Eye, was possessed in a remarkable degree by learned and wise people, especially poets, so that they could make themselves loved and followed by any girl they liked, simply by the influence of the glance. About the year 1790, a young man resided in the County of Limerick, who had this power in a singular and unusual degree. He was a clever, witty rhymer in the Irish language; and, probably, had the deep poet eyes that characterize warm and passionate poet-natures—eyes that even without necromancy have been known to exercise a powerful magnetic influence over female minds.

One day, while travelling far from home, he came upon a bright, pleasant-looking farmhouse, and feeling weary, he stopped and requested a drink of milk and leave to rest. The farmer's daughter, a young, handsome girl, not liking to admit a stranger, as all the maids were churning, and she was alone in the house, refused him admittance.

The young poet fixed his eyes earnestly on her face for some time in silence, then slowly turning round left the house, and walked towards a small grove of trees just opposite. There he stood for a few moments resting against a tree, and facing the house as if to take one last vengeful or admiring glance, then went his way without once turning round.

The young girl had been watching him from the windows, and the moment he moved she passed out of the door like one in a dream, and followed him slowly, step by step, down the avenue. The maids grew alarmed, and called to her father, who ran out and shouted loudly for her to stop, but she never turned or seemed to heed. The young man, however, looked round, and seeing the whole family in pursuit, quickened his pace, first glancing fixedly at the girl for a moment. Immediately she sprang towards him, and they were both almost out of sight, when one of the maids espied a piece of paper tied to a branch of the tree where the poet had rested. From curiosity she took it down, and the moment the knot was untied, the farmer's daughter suddenly stopped, became quite still, and when her father came up she allowed him to lead her back to the house without resistance.

When questioned, she said that she felt herself drawn by an invisible force to follow the young stranger wherever he might lead, and that she would have followed him through the world, for her life seemed to be bound up in his; she had no will to resist, and was conscious of nothing else but his presence. Suddenly, however, the spell was broken, and then she heard her father's voice, and knew how strangely she had acted. At the same time the power of the young man over her vanished, and the impulse to follow him was no longer in her heart.

The paper, on being opened, was found to contain five mysterious words written in blood, and in this order—

Sator.

Arepo.

Tenet.

Opera.

Rotas.

These letters are so arranged that read in any way, right to left, left to right, up or down, the same words are produced; and when written in blood with a pen made of an eagle's feather, they form a charm which no woman (it is said) can resist; but the incredulous reader can easily test the truth of this assertion for himself.

TRUE IRISH GHOST STORIES

John D. Seymore

HAUNTED HOUSES IN OR NEAR DUBLIN

OF all species of ghostly phenomena, that commonly known as "haunted houses" appeals most to the ordinary person. There is something very eerie in being shut up within the four walls of a house with a ghost. The poor human being is placed at such a disadvantage. If we know that a gateway, or road, or field has the reputation of being haunted, we can in nearly every case make a detour, and so avoid the unpleasant locality. But the presence of a ghost in a house creates a very different state of affairs. It appears and disappears at its own sweet will, with a total disregard for our feelings: it seems to be as much part and parcel of the domicile as the staircase or the hall door, and, consequently, nothing short of leaving the house or of pulling it down (both of these solutions are not always practicable) will free us absolutely from the unwelcome presence.

There is also something so natural, and at the same time so unnatural, in seeing a door open when we know that no human hand rests on the knob, or in hearing the sound of footsteps, light or heavy, and feeling that it cannot be attributed to the feet of mortal man or woman. Or perhaps a form appears in a room, standing, sitting, or walking—in fact, situated in its three dimensions apparently as an ordinary being of flesh and blood, until it proves its unearthly nature by vanishing before our astonished eyes. Or perhaps we are asleep in bed. The room is shrouded in darkness, and our recumbent attitude, together with the weight of bed-clothes, hampers our movements and probably makes us more cowardly. A man will meet pain or danger boldly if he be standing upright—occupying that erect position which is his as Lord of Creation; but his courage does not well so high if he be supine. We are awakened suddenly by the feel that some superhuman Presence is in the room. We are transfixed with terror, we cannot find either the bell-rope or the matches, while we *dare* not leap out of bed and make a rush for the door lest we should encounter we know not what. In an agony of fear, we feel it moving towards us; it approaches closer, and yet closer, to the bed, and—for what may or may not then happen we must refer our readers to the pages of this book.

But the sceptical reader will say: "This is all very well, but—there are *no* haunted houses. All these alleged strange happenings are due to a vivid imagination, or else to rats and mice." (The question of deliberate and conscious fraud may be rejected in almost every instance.) This simple solution has been put forward so often that it should infallibly have solved the problem long ago. But will such a reader explain how it is that the noise made by rats and mice can resemble slow, heavy footsteps, or else take the form of a human being seen by several persons; or how our imagination can cause doors to open and shut, or else create a conglomeration of noises which, physically, would be beyond the power of ordinary individuals to reproduce? Whatever may be the ultimate explanation, we feel that there is a great deal in the words quoted by Professor Barrett: "In spite of all reasonable scepticism, it is difficult to avoid accepting, at least provisionally, the conclusion that there are, in a certain sense, haunted houses, *i.e.* that there are houses in which similar quasi-human apparitions have occurred at different times to different inhabitants, under circumstances which exclude the hypothesis of suggestion or expectation."

We must now turn to the subject of this chapter. Mrs. G. Kelly, a lady well known in musical circles in Dublin, sends as her own personal experience the following tale of a most quiet haunting, in which the spectral charwoman (!) does not seem to have entirely laid aside all her mundane habits.

"My first encounter with a ghost occurred about twenty years ago. On that occasion I was standing in the kitchen of my house in——Square, when a woman, whom I was afterwards to see many times, walked down the stairs into the room. Having heard the footsteps outside, I was not in the least perturbed, but turned to look who it was, and found myself looking at a tall, stout, elderly woman, wearing a bonnet and old-fashioned mantle. She had grey hair and a benign and amiable expression. We stood gazing at each other while one could Count twenty. At first I was not at all frightened, but gradually as I stood looking at her an uncomfortable feeling, increasing to terror, came over me. This caused me to retreat farther and farther back, until I had my back against the wall, and then the apparition slowly faded.

"This feeling of terror, due perhaps to the unexpectedness of her appearance, always overcame me on the subsequent occasions on which I saw her. These occasions numbered twelve or fifteen, and I have seen her in every room in the house, and at every hour of the day, during a period of about ten years. The last time she appeared was ten years ago. My husband and I had just returned from a concert at which he had been singing, and we sat for some time over supper, talking about the events of the evening. When at last I rose to leave the room, and opened the dining-room door, I found my old lady standing on the mat outside with her head bent towards the door in the attitude of listening. I called out loudly, and my husband rushed to my side. That was the last time I have seen her.

"One peculiarity of this spectral visitant was a strong objection to disorder or untidiness of any kind, or even to an alteration in the general routine of the house. For instance, she showed her disapproval of any stranger coming to sleep by turning the chairs face downwards on the floor in the room they were to occupy. I well remember one of our guests, having gone to his room one evening for something he had forgotten, remarking on coming downstairs again, 'Well, you people have an extraordinary manner of arranging your furniture! I have nearly broken my bones over one of the bedroom chairs which was turned down on the floor.' As my husband and I had restored that chair twice already to its proper position during the day, we were not much surprised at his remarks, although we did not enlighten him. The whole family have been disturbed by a peculiar knocking which occurred in various rooms in the house, frequently on the door or wall, but sometimes on the furniture, quite close to where we had been sitting. This was evidently loud enough to be heard in the next house, for our next-door neighbour once asked my husband why he selected such curious hours for hanging his pictures. Another strange and fairly frequent occurrence was the following. I had got a set of skunk furs which I fancied had an unpleasant odour, as this fur sometimes has; and at night I used to take it from my wardrobe and lay it on a chair in the drawing-room, which was next my bedroom. The first time that I did this, on going to the drawing-room I found, to my surprise, my muff in one corner and my stole in another. Not for a moment suspecting a supernatural agent, I asked my servant about it, and she assured me that she had not been in the room that morning. Whereupon I determined to test the matter, which I did by putting in the furs late at night, and taking care that I was the first to enter the room in the morning. I invariably found that they had been disturbed."

A most weird experience fell to the lot of Major Macgregor, and was contributed by him to *Real Ghost Stories*, the celebrated Christmas number of the *Review of Reviews*. He says: "In the end of 1871 I went over to Ireland to visit a relative living in a Square in the north side of Dublin. In January 1872 the husband of my relative fell ill. I sat up with him for several nights, and at last, as he seemed better, I went to bed, and directed the footman to call me if anything went wrong. I soon fell asleep, but some time after was awakened by a push on the left shoulder. I started up, and said, 'Is there anything wrong?' I got no answer, but immediately received another push. I got annoyed, and said, 'Can you not speak, man! and tell me if there is anything wrong?' Still no answer, and I had a feeling I was going to get another push when I suddenly turned round and caught a human hand, warm, plump, and soft. I said, 'Who are you?' but I got no answer. I then tried to pull the person towards me, but could not do so. I then said, 'I *will* know who you are!' and having the hand tight in my right hand, with my left I felt the wrist and arm, enclosed, as it seemed to me, in a tight-fitting sleeve of some winter material with a linen cuff, but when I got to the elbow all trace of an arm ceased. I was so astounded that I let the hand go, and just then the clock struck two. Including the mistress of the house, there were five females in the establishment, and I can assert that the hand belonged to none of them. When I reported the adventure, the servants exclaimed, 'Oh, it must have been the master's old Aunt Betty, who lived for many years in the upper part of that house, and had died over fifty years before at a great age.' I afterwards heard that the room in which I felt the hand had been considered haunted, and very curious noises and peculiar incidents occurred, such as the bedclothes torn off, etc. One lady got a slap in the face from some invisible hand, and when she lit her candle she saw as if something opaque fell or jumped off the bed. A general officer, a brother of the lady, slept there two nights, but preferred going to a hotel to remaining the third night. He never would say what he heard or saw, but always said the room was uncanny. I slept for months in the room afterwards, and was never in the least disturbed."

A truly terrifying sight was. witnessed by a clergyman in a schoolhouse a good many years ago. This cleric was curate of a Dublin parish, but resided with his parents some distance out of town in the direction of Malahide. It not infrequently happened that he had to hold meetings in the evenings, and on such occasions, as his home was so far away, and as the modern convenience of tramcars was not then known, he used to sleep in the schoolroom, a large bare room, where the meetings were held. He had made a sleeping-apartment for himself by placing a pole across one end of the room, on which he had rigged up two curtains which, when drawn together, met in the middle. One night he had been holding some meeting, and when everybody had left he locked up the empty schoolhouse and went to bed. It was a bright moonlight night, and every object could be seen perfectly clearly. Scarcely had he got into bed when be became conscious of some invisible presence. Then he saw the curtains agitated at one end, as if hands were grasping them on the outside. In an agony of terror he watched these hands groping along outside the curtains till they reached the middle. The curtains were then drawn a little apart, and a Face peered in—an awful, evil Face, with an expression of wickedness and hate upon it which no words could describe. It looked at him for a few moments, then drew back again, and the curtains closed. The clergyman had sufficient courage left to leap out of bed and make a thorough examination of the room, but, as he expected, he found no one. He dressed himself as quickly as possible, walked home, and never again slept a night in that schoolroom.

The following tale, sent by Mr. E. B. de Lacy, contains a most extraordinary and unsatisfactory element of mystery. He says: "When I was a boy I lived in the suburbs, and used to come in every morning to school, in the city. My way lay through a certain street in which stood a very dismal semi-detached house, which, I might say, was closed up regularly about every six months. I would see new tenants coming into it, and then in a few months it would be 'To let' again. This went on for eight or nine years, and I often wondered what was the reason. On inquiring one day from a friend, I was told that it had the reputation of being haunted.

"A few years later I entered business in a certain office, and one day it fell to my lot to have to call on the lady who at that particular period was the tenant of the haunted house. When we had transacted our business she informed me that she was about to leave. Knowing the reputation of the house, and being desirous of investigating a ghost-story,

I asked her if she would give me the history of the house as far as she knew it, which she very kindly did as follows:

"About forty years ago the house was left by will to a gentleman named——. He lived in it for a short time, when he suddenly went mad, and had to be put in an asylum. Upon this his agents let the house to a lady. Apparently nothing unusual happened for some time, but a few months later, as she went down one morning to a room behind the kitchen, she found the cook hanging by a rope attached to a hook in the ceiling. After the inquest the lady gave up the house.

"It was then closed up for some time, but was again advertised 'To let', and a caretaker, a woman, was put into it. One night about one o'clock, a constable going his rounds heard some one calling for help from the house, and found the caretaker on the sill of one of the windows holding on as best she could. He told her to go in and open the hall door and let him in, but she refused to enter the room again. He forced open the door and succeeded in dragging the woman back into the room, only to find she had gone mad.

"Again the house was shut up, and again it was let, this time to a lady, on a five-years' lease. However, after a few months' residence, she locked it up, and went away. On her friends asking her why she did so, she replied that she would rather pay the whole five years' rent than live in it herself, or allow any one else to do so, but would give no other reason.

" 'I believe I was the next person to take this house,' said the lady who narrated the story to me (*i.e.* Mr. de Lacy). 'I took it about eighteen months ago on a three years' lease, in the hopes of making money by taking in boarders, but I am now giving it up because none of them will stay more than a week or two. They do not give any definite reason as to why they are leaving; they are careful to state that it is not because they have any fault to find with me or my domestic arrangements, but they merely say *they do not like the rooms*! The rooms themselves, as you can see, are good, spacious, and well lighted. I have had all classes of professional men; one of the last was a barrister, and he said that he had no fault to find except that *he did not like the rooms*! I myself do not believe in ghosts, and I have never seen anything strange here or elsewhere; and if I had known the house had the reputation of being haunted, I would never have rented it.' "

Marsh's library, that quaint, old-world repository of ponderous tomes, is reputed to be haunted by the ghost of its founder, Primate Narcissus Marsh. He is said to frequent the inner gallery, which contains what was formerly his own private library: he moves in and out among the cases, taking down books from the shelves, and occasionally throwing them down on the reader's desk as if in anger. However, he always leaves things in perfect order. The late Mr.——, who for some years lived in the librarian's rooms underneath, was a firm believer in this ghost, and said he frequently heard noises which could only be accounted for by the presence of a nocturnal visitor; the present tenant is more sceptical. The story goes that Marsh's niece eloped from the palace, and was married in a tavern to the curate of Chapelizod. She is reported to have written a note consenting to the elopement, and to have then placed it in one of her uncle's books to which her lover had access, and where he found it. As a punishment for his lack of vigilance, the Archbishop is said to be condemned to hunt for the note until he find it—hence the ghost.

The ghost of a deceased Canon was seen in one of the Dublin cathedrals by several independent witnesses, one of whom, a lady, gives her own experience as follows: "Canon——was a personal friend of mine, and we had many times discussed ghosts and spiritualism, in which he was a profound believer, having had many supernatural experiences himself. It was during the Sunday morning service in the cathedral that I saw my friend, who had been dead for two years, sitting inside the communion-rails. I was so much astonished at the flesh-and-blood appearance of the figure that I took off my glasses and wiped them with my handkerchief, at the same time looking away from him down the church. On looking back again he was still there, and continued to sit there for about ten or twelve minutes, after which he faded away. I remarked a change in his personal appearance, which was, that his beard was longer and whiter than when I had known him—in fact, such a change as would have occurred *in life* in the space of two years. Having told my husband of the occurrence on our way home, he remembered having heard some talk of an appearance of this clergyman in the cathedral since his death. He hurried back to the afternoon service, and asked the robestress if anybody had seen Canon——'s ghost. She informed him that *she* had, and that he had also been seen by one of the sextons in the cathedral. I mention this because in describing his personal appearance she had remarked the same change as I had with regard to the beard."

Some years ago a family had very uncanny experiences in a house in Rathgar, and subsequently in another in Rathmines. These were communicated by one of the young ladies to Mrs. M. A. Wilkins, who published them in the *Journal of the American S.P.R.*,[1] from which they are here taken. The Rathgar house had a basement passage leading to a door into the yard, and along this passage her mother and the children used to hear dragging, limping steps, and the latch of the door rattling, but no one could ever be found when search was made. The house-bells were old and all in a row, and on one occasion they all rang, apparently of their own accord. The lady narrator used to sleep in the back drawing-room, and always when the light was put out she heard strange noises, as if some one was going round the room rubbing paper along the wall, while she often had the feeling that a person was standing beside her bed. A cousin, who was a nurse, once slept with her, and also noticed these strange noises. On one occasion this room was given up to a very matter-of-fact young man to sleep in, and next morning he said that the room was very strange, with queer noises in it.

Her mother also had an extraordinary experience in the same house. One evening she had just put the baby to bed, when she heard a voice calling "mother ". She left the bedroom, and called to her daughter, who was in a lower room, "What do you want?" But the girl replied that she had *not* called her; and then, in her turn, asked her mother if *she* had been in the front room, for she had just heard a noise as if some one was trying to fasten the inside bars of the shutters across. But her mother had been upstairs, and no one was in the front room. The experiences in the Rathmines house were of a similar auditory nature, *i.e.* the young ladies heard their names called, though it was found that no one in the house had done so.

Occasionally it happens that ghosts inspire a law-suit. In

the seventeenth century they were to be found actively urging the adoption of legal proceedings, but in the nineteenth and twentieth centuries they play a more passive part. A case about a haunted house took place in Dublin in the year 1885, in which the ghost may be said to have won. A Mr. Waldron, a solicitor's clerk, sued his next-door neighbour, one Mr. Kiernan, a mate in the merchant service, to recover £500 for damages done to his house.

Kiernan altogether denied the charges, but asserted that Waldron's house was notoriously haunted. Witnesses proved that every night, from August 1884 to January 1885, stones were thrown at the windows and doors, and extraordinary and inexplicable occurrences constantly took place.

Mrs. Waldron, wife of the plaintiff, swore that one night she saw one of the panes of glass of a certain window cut through with a diamond, and a white hand inserted through the hole. She at once caught up a bill-hook and aimed a blow at the hand, cutting off one of the fingers. This finger could not be found, nor were any traces of blood seen.

A servant of hers was sorely persecuted by noises and the sound of footsteps. Mr. Waldron, with the aid of detectives and policemen, endeavoured to find out the cause, but with no success. The witnesses in the case were closely cross-examined, but without shaking their testimony. The facts appeared to be proved, so the jury found for Kiernan, the defendant. At least twenty persons had testified on oath to the fact that the house had been known to have been haunted.[1]

Before leaving the city and its immediate surroundings, we must relate the story of an extraordinary ghost, somewhat lacking in good manners, yet not without a certain distorted sense of humour. Absolutely incredible though the tale may seem, yet it comes on very good authority. It was related to our informant, Mr. D., by a Mrs. C., whose daughter he had employed as governess. Mrs. C., who is described as "a woman of respectable position and good education", heard it in her turn from her father and mother. In the story the relationship of the different persons seems a little involved, but it would appear that the initial A belongs to the surname both of Mrs. C.'s father and grandfather.

This ghost was commonly called "Corney" by the family, and he answered to this though it was not his proper name. He disclosed this latter to Mr. C.'s mother, who forgot it. Corney made his presence manifest to the A. family shortly after they had gone to reside in——Street in the following manner. Mr. A. had sprained his knee badly, and had to use a crutch, which at night was left at the head of his bed. One night his wife heard some one walking on the lobby, thump, thump, thump, as if imitating Mr. A. She struck a match to see if the crutch had been removed from the head of the bed, but it was still there.

From that on Corney commenced to talk, and he spoke every day from his usual habitat, the coal-cellar off the kitchen. His voice sounded as if it came out of an empty barrel.

He was very troublesome, and continually played practical jokes on the servants, who, as might be expected, were in terror of their lives of him; so much so that Mrs. A. could hardly induce them to stay with her. They used to sleep in a press-bed in the kitchen, and in order to get away from Corney, they asked for a room at the top of the house, which was given to them. Accordingly the press-bed was moved up there. The first night they went to retire to bed after the change, the doors of the press were flung open, and Corney's voice said, "Ha! ha! you devils, I am here before you! I am not confined to any particular part of this house."

Corney was continually tampering with the doors, and straining locks and keys. He only manifested himself in material form to two persons; to——, who died with the fright, and to Mr. A. (Mrs. C.'s father) when he was about seven years old. The latter described him to his mother as a naked man, with a curl on his forehead, and a skin like a clothes-horse (!).

One day a servant was preparing fish for dinner. She laid it on the kitchen table while she went elsewhere for something she wanted. When she returned the fish had disappeared. She thereupon began to cry, fearing she would be accused of making away with it. The next thing she heard was the voice of Corney from the coal-cellar saying, "There, you blubbering fool, is your fish for you!" and, suiting the action to the word, the fish was thrown out on the kitchen floor.

Relatives from the country used to bring presents of vegetables, and these were often hung up by Corney like Christmas decorations round the kitchen. There was one particular press in the kitchen he would not allow anything into. He would throw it out again. A crock with meat in pickle was put into it, and a fish placed on the cover of the crock. He threw the fish out.

Silver teaspoons were missing, and no account of them could be got, until Mrs. A. asked Corney to confess if he had done anything with them. He said, "They are under the ticking in the servants' bed." He had, so he said, a daughter in——Street, and sometimes announced that he was going to see her, and would not be here tonight.

On one occasion he announced that he was going to have "company" that evening, and if they wanted any water out of the soft-water tank, to take it before going to bed, as he and his friends would be using it. Subsequently that night five or six distinct voices were heard, and next morning the water in the tank was as black as ink, and not alone that, but the bread and butter in the pantry were streaked with the marks of sooty fingers.

A clergyman in the locality, having heard of the doings of Corney, called to investigate the matter. He was advised by Mrs. A. to keep quiet, and not to reveal his identity, as being the best chance of hearing Corney speak. He waited a long time, and as the capricious Corney remained silent, he left at length. The servants asked, "Corney, why did you not speak?" and he replied, "I could not speak while that good man was in the house." The servants sometimes used to ask him where he was. He would reply, "The Great God would not permit me to tell you. I was a bad man, and I died the death." He named the room in the house in which he died.

Corney constantly joined in any conversation carried on by the people of the house. One could never tell when a voice from the coal-cellar would erupt into the dialogue. He had his likes and dislikes; he appeared to dislike any one that was not afraid of him, and would not talk to them. Mrs. C.'s mother, however, used to get good of him by coaxing. An uncle, having failed to get him to speak one night, took the kitchen poker, and hammered at the door of the coal-cellar, saying, "I'll make you speak"; but Corney wouldn't. Next morning the poker was found broken in two. This uncle used to wear spectacles, and Corney used to call him derisively, "Four-eyes". An uncle named Richard came to sleep one night, and complained in the morning that the clothes were pulled off him. Corney told the servants in great glee, "I slept on Master Richard's feet all night."

Finally Mr. A. made several attempts to dispose of his lease, but with no success, for when intending purchasers were being shown over the house and arrived at Corney's domain, the spirit would begin to speak and the would-be purchaser would fly. They asked him if they changed house would he trouble them. He replied, "No! but if they throw down this house, I will trouble the stones."

At last Mrs. A. appealed to him to keep quiet, and not to injure people who had never injured him. He promised that he would do so, and then said, "Mrs. A., you will be all right now, for I see a lady in black coming up the street to this house, and she will buy it." Within half an hour a widow called and purchased the house. Possibly Corney is still there, for our informant looked up the Directory as he was writing, and found the house marked "Vacant".

Near Blanchardstown, Co. Dublin, is a house, occupied at present, or up to very recently, by a private family; it was formerly a monastery, and there are said to be secret passages in it. Once a servant ironing in the kitchen saw the figure of a nun approach the kitchen window and look in. Our informant was also told by a friend (now dead), who had it from the lady of the house, that once night falls, no doors can be kept closed. If any one shuts them, almost immediately they are flung open again with the greatest violence and apparent anger. If left open there is no trouble or noise, but light footsteps are heard, and there is a vague feeling of people passing to and fro. The persons inhabiting the house are matter-of-fact, unimaginative people, who speak of this as if it were an everyday affair. "So long as we leave the doors unclosed they don't harm us: why should we be afraid of them?" Mrs.——said. Truly a most philosophical attitude to adopt!

A haunted house in Kingstown, Co. Dublin, was investigated by Professor W. Barrett and Professor Henry Sidgwick. The story is singularly well attested (as one might expect from its being inserted in the pages of the *Proceedings S.P.R.*[1]), as the apparition was seen on three distinct occasions, and by three separate persons who were all personally known to the above gentlemen. The house in which the following occurrences took place is described as being a very old one, with unusually thick walls. The lady saw her strange visitant in her bedroom. She says: "Disliking cross-lights, I had got into the habit of having the blind of the back window drawn and the shutters closed at night, and of leaving the blind raised and the shutters opened towards the front, liking to see the trees and sky when I awakened. Opening my eyes now one morning, I saw right before me (this occurred in July

1873) the figure of a woman, stooping down and apparently looking at me. Her head and shoulders were wrapped in a common woollen shawl; her arms were folded, and they were also wrapped, as if for warmth, in the shawl. I looked at her in my horror, and dared not cry out lest I might move the awful thing to speech or action. Behind her head I saw the window and the growing dawn, the looking-glass upon the toilet-table, and the furniture in that part of the room. After what may have been only seconds—of the duration of this vision I cannot judge—she raised herself and went backwards towards the window, stood at the toilet-table, and gradually vanished. I mean she grew by degrees transparent, and that through the shawl and the grey dress she wore I saw the white muslin of the table-cover again, and at last saw that only in the place where she had stood." The lady lay motionless with terror until the servant came to call her. The only other occupants of the house at the time were her brother and the servant, to neither of whom did she make any mention of the circumstance, fearing that the former would laugh at her, and the latter give notice.

Exactly a fortnight later, when sitting at breakfast, she noticed that her brother seemed out of sorts, and did not eat. On asking him if anything were the matter, he answered, "I have had a horrid nightmare—indeed it was no nightmare: I saw it early this morning, just as distinctly as I see you."

"What?" she asked. "A villainous-looking hag," he replied, "with her head and arms wrapped in a cloak, stooping over me, and looking like this——" He got up, folded his arms, and put himself in the exact posture of the vision. Whereupon she informed him of what she herself had seen a fortnight previously.

About four years later, in the same month, the lady's married sister and two children were alone in the house. The eldest child, a boy of about four or five years, asked for a drink, and his mother went to fetch it, desiring him to remain in the dining-room until her return. Coming back she met the boy pale and trembling, and on asking him why he left the room, he replied, "Who is that woman—who is that woman?" "Where?" she asked. "That old woman who went upstairs," he replied. So agitated was he, that she took him by the hand and went upstairs to search, but no one was to be found, though he still maintained that a woman went upstairs. A friend of the family subsequently told them that a woman had been killed in the house many years previously, and that it was reported to be haunted.

A lady sends a very curious account of the appearance of an archiepiscopal ghost in a house in the outskirts of Dublin. Those of my readers who are acquainted with that Archbishop's family history will be able to say if some of the facts related below are correct.

A good many years ago a Mrs. P., an intimate friend of the narrator, lived in Upper Fitzwilliam Street. Her husband had held the post of Government arbitrator, and was subsequently agent to a large estate. During his lifetime he and his wife resided at a house near Dundrum, Co. Dublin, a great rambling old mansion, which has since suffered the fate of so many stately houses, as it has become a teaching establishment of some sort.

One afternoon, when it was getting dusk, Mrs. P. was descending the large staircase when she saw going down before her what she imagined to be her youngest son, W., curiously attired. She had three sons, all of whom were very fond of amateur theatricals, and from the dress that W. wore she thought that he was about to take part in some rehearsal. He was clad in a large broad-brimmed sombrero, and a cloak put on in Spanish, fashion. She called to him by name, bidding him wait for her, but to her surprise he took absolutely no notice, but continued descending, she following him, until he reached the door of the dining-room, which he entered. She was quite annoyed at his want of manners, and followed him into the dining-room, an apartment which they did not always use because it was very large. To her utter astonishment she found herself confronted, not by her son, but by an utter stranger who had walked to the far side of the dining-table, and there stood facing her. His cloak was pulled up so as to cover his mouth, and his hat drawn well down over his face, and on this account Mrs. P. was unable to distinguish his features, but she could see that his eyes were looking at her. Then he walked a little round the table, and suddenly vanished. Mrs. P. got a great shock, but her sons, when they heard it, attributed it to imagination pure and simple.

"I had heard this story many times, and never paid much heed to it," continued our narrator. "However, one day I went to a Loreto Convent to visit some nuns of my acquaintance who were there for their holidays, and while there the conversation turned on the subject of ghosts. I related the story I have just told to you. One of the nuns present asked if she might bring in another nun to hear the story; this latter was a Rev. Mother of an English House who was over for her holiday. I was quite agreeable, so this Rev. Mother was introduced, and to her I told my tale again. She seemed more than usually interested, and said she would particularly like to meet Mrs. P., if it were possible, and would I ask her to try and recall the exact day and date on which she had seen the figure in the dining-room.

"I made an arrangement with Mrs. P., and brought her to the convent, where she met this Rev. Mother, to whom she related her experience, giving day and date, and almost the exact hour. From the subsequent conversation I learnt that this Rev. Mother was a niece, or some near relative, of the celebrated Archbishop Whately; she had turned Roman Catholic, and had entered a Loreto Convent. The Archbishop had owned this old mansion where Mrs. P. had lived, and had resided there for some time. It was said that he used to appear there whenever any near relative of his died. On ascertaining the day and date of the appearance to Mrs. P., the Rev. Mother was able to say that exactly at that time her cousin, a daughter (I think) of the Archbishop's, had passed away. He had been in Spain, and had brought back from there the sombrero and cloak which he fancied very much. Thus the theatrically-clad figure which was seen by my friend was none other than the Archbishop himself."

A much more unpleasant haunting was experienced by Mrs. E.H.B. and her daughters in a house on the south side of Dublin.[1]

"This house was a large, sunny, rambling old place, not the least like the typical 'haunted house'. Our two girls occupied a very large room at the back of the house, little F. being a hopeless invalid, and needing some one to sleep in her room.

"We had been there about a week, and we had just gone to bed, when M. (our eldest girl) rushed wildly into our room crying: 'Mother, there is something rushing about in our bedroom, and we can't see it, and F. is so frightened—do come!'

"I ran down at once, and on the stairs I could distinctly hear something jumping about in their room, the door of which was open. Before we got in, however, the noise stopped, but I promised I would stay with them all night, for poor little F. could not speak, and clung to me convulsively.

"At last all was quiet, the girls slept, when I heard in one corner of the room a soft, sighing, whispering sound, which seemed to come out of the wall, and gradually crept all round the room till it reached where our beds were. Nearer it came, till it touched the bed, as if a winged beetle were fluttering against the quilt. All at once something heavy seemed to fall, and immediately the footfalls I had heard before sounded with a peculiar hollow thud, as if some animal (cat or dog) were jumping up and down; it lasted about ten minutes, and suddenly died away at the door. Next morning both girls exactly described the first part of the noise as I had heard it, and it always came in the same way—an indescribable whisper in the beginning, and the conclusion a heavy thud.

"But next day we had a visit from a friend (!), a pet aversion of ours, whose presence always put little sensitive F. into a fever. I subsequently noticed that whenever this person came to see us we always received a visit overnight from the 'Prone' (a name that F. gave to the 'thuddy' sounds of our ghost), as if it knew that some evil was on its way to us, and was drawn to the spot by its magnetic influence. Indeed after a visit from the 'Pronc' I always stayed in next day to be on the spot and protect the children.

"One evening I was sitting in the firelight by F.'s bed, telling her stories, as I often did, when she gripped my hand, and nodded towards the fire. I looked round. There on the rug, with its back to us, sat a black animal, like a large tomcat, gazing into the fire! I thought it was F.'s pet cat, and called out, 'Well, Peter-Puss! Are you come in for your supper?' The creature turned, and looked full at us for a moment with *eyes that were human*, and a face which, though black, was still the face of an *ugly woman*! The mouth snarled at us for an instant, and a sad, angry howl came from it; and as we stared in horror, the thing vanished. We never saw it again, but the strain was too much, and we left the house as soon as we could. We were told later that fifty years before a woman had been robbed and murdered in that room by her son, and buried by him under the hearthstone! Twenty years after, her skeleton , was found by tenants, who, troubled by the ghost, searched the house, and gave their gruesome find decent burial."

[1] For September 1913.

[1] See *Sights and Shadows*, p. 42 ff.

[1] July 1884, p. 141.

THE DUALITISTS

Bram Stoker

1

BIS DAT QUI NON CITO DAT

There was joy in the house of Bubb. For ten long years had Ephraim and Sophonisba Bubb mourned in vain the loneliness of their life. Unavailingly had they gazed into the emporia of baby-linen, and fixed their searching glances on the basket-makers' warehouses where the cradles hung in tempting rows. In vain had they prayed, and sighed, and groaned, and wished, and waited, and wept, but never had even a ray of hope been held out by the family physician.

But now at last the wished-for moment had arrived. Month after month had flown by on leaden wings, and the destined days had slowly measured their course. The months had become weeks; the weeks had dwindled down to days; the days had been attenuated to hours; the hours had lapsed into minutes, the minutes had slowly died away, and but seconds remained.

Ephraim Bubb sat cowering on the stairs, and tried with high-strung ears to catch the strain of blissful music from the lips of his first-born. There was silence in the house – silence as of the deadly calm before the cyclone. Ah! Ephraim Bubb, little thinkest thou that another moment may for ever destroy the peaceful, happy course of thy life, and open to thy too-craving eyes the portals of that wondrous land where childhood reigns supreme, and where the tyrant infant with the wave of his tiny hand and the imperious treble of his tiny voice sentences his parent to the deadly vault beneath the castle moat. As the thought strikes thee thou becomest pale. How thou tremblest as thou findest thyself upon the brink of the abyss! Wouldst that thou could recall the past!

But hark! the die is cast for good or ill. The long years

of praying and hoping have found an end at last. From the chamber within comes a sharp cry, which shordy after is repeated. Ah! Ephraim, that cry is the feeble effort of childish lips as yet unused to the rough, worldly form of speech to frame the word 'father'. In the glow of thy transport all doubts are forgotten; and when the doctor cometh forth as the harbinger of joy he findeth thee radiant with new-found delight.

'My dear sir, allow me to congratulate you – to offer twofold felicitations. Mr Bubb, sir, you are the father of twins!'

2

HALCYON DAYS

The twins were the finest children that ever were seen–so at least said the *cognoscenti*, and the parents were not slow to believe. The nurse's opinion was in itself a proof.

It was not, ma'am, that they was fine for twins, but they was fine for singles, and she had ought to know, for she had nussed a many in her time, both twins *and* singles. All they wanted was to have their dear little legs cut off and little wings on their dear little shoulders, for to be put one on each side of a white marble tombstone, cut beautiful, sacred to the relic of Ephraim Bubb, that they might, sir, if so be that missus was to survive the father of two such lovely twins–although she would make bold to say, and no offence intended, that a handsome gentleman, though a trifle or two older than his good lady, though for the matter of that she heerd that gentlemen was never too old at all, and for her own part she liked them the better for it: not like bits of boys that didn't know their own minds–that a gentleman what was the father of two such 'eavenly twins (God bless them!) couldn't be called anything but a boy; though for the matter of that she never knowed in her experience–which it was much–of a boy as had such twins, or any twins at all so much for the matter of that.

The twins were the idols of their parents, and at the same time their pleasure and their pain. Did Zerubbabel cough, Ephraim would start from his balmy slumbers with an agonized cry of consternation, for visions of innumerable twins black in the face from croup haunted his nightly pillow. Did Zacariah rail at ethereal expansion, Sophonisba with pallid hue and dishevelled locks would fly to the cradle of her offspring. Did pins torture or strings afflict, or flannel or flies tickle, or light dazzle, or darkness affright, or hunger or thirst assail the synchronous productions, the household of Bubb would be roused from quiet slumbers or the current of its manifold workings changed.

The twins grew apace; were weaned; teethed; and at length arrived at the stage of three years!

They grew in beauty side by side,

They filled one home, *etc.*

3

RUMOURS OF WARS

Harry Merford and Tommy Santon lived in the same range of villas as Ephraim Bubb. Harry's parents had taken up their abode in no. 25, no. 27 was happy in the perpetual sunshine of Tommy's smiles, and between these two residences Ephraim Bubb reared his blossoms, the number of his mansion being 26. Harry and Tommy had been accustomed from the earliest times to meet each other daily. Their primal method of communication had been by the housetops, till their respective sires had been obliged to pay compensation to Bubb for damages to his roof and dormer windows; and from that time they had been forbidden by the home authorities to meet, whilst their mutual neighbour had taken the precaution of having his garden walls pebble-dashed and topped with broken glass to prevent their incursions. Harry and Tommy, however, being gifted with daring souls, lofty, ambitious, impetuous natures, and strong seats to their trousers, defied the rugged walls of Bubb and continued to meet in secret.

Compared with these two youths, Castor and Pollux, Damon and Pythias, Eloisa and Abelard are but tame examples of duality or constancy and friendship. All the poets from Hyginus to Schiller might sing of noble deeds and desperate dangers held as naught for friendship's sake, but they would have been mute had they but known of the mutual affection of Harry and Tommy. Day by day, and often night by night, would these two brave the perils of nurse, and father, and mother, of whip and imprisonment, and hunger and thirst, and solitude and darkness to meet together. What they discussed in secret none other knew. What deeds of darkness were perpetrated in their symposia none could tell. Alone they met, alone they remained, and alone they departed to their several abodes. There was in the garden of Bubb a summer-house overgrown with trailing plants, and surrounded by young poplars which the fond father had planted on his children's natal day, and whose rapid growth he had proudly watched. These trees quite obscured the summer-house, and here Harry and Tommy, knowing after a careful observation that none ever entered the place, held their conclaves. Time after time they met in full security and followed their customary pursuit of pleasure. Let us raise the mysterious veil and see what was the great Unknown at whose shrine they bent the knee.

Harry and Tommy had each been given as a Christmas box a new knife; and for a long time–nearly a year–these knives, similar in size and pattern, were their chief delights. With them they cut and hacked in their respective homes all things which would not be likely to be noticed; for the young gentlemen were wary and had no wish that their moments of pleasure should be atoned for by moments of pain. The insides of drawers, and desks, and boxes, the underparts of tables and chairs, the backs of pictures frames, even the floors, where corners of the carpets could surreptitiously be turned up, all bore marks of their craftsmanship; and to compare notes on these artistic triumphs was a source of joy. At length, however, a critical time came, some new field of action should be opened up, for the old appetites were sated, and the old joys had begun to pall. It was absolutely necessary that the existing schemes of destruction should be enlarged; and yet this could hardly be done without a terrible risk of discovery, for the limits of safety had long since been reached and passed. But, be the risk great or small, some new ground should be broken—some new joy found, for the old earth was barren, and the craving for pleasure was growing fiercer with each successive day.

The crisis had come: who could tell the issue?

4

THE TUCKET SOUNDS

They met in the arbour, determined to discuss this grave question. The heart of each was big with revolution, the head of each was full of scheme and strategy, and the pocket of each was full of sweet-stuff, the sweeter for being stolen. After having dispatched the sweets, the conspirators proceeded to explain their respective views with regard to the enlargement of their artistic operations. Tommy unfolded with much pride a scheme which he had in contemplation of cutting a series of holes in the sounding board of the piano, so as to destroy its musical properties. Harry was in no wise behindhand in his ideas of reform. He had conceived the project of cutting the canvas at the back of his great-grandfather's portrait, which his father held in high regard among his lares and penates, so that in time when the picture should be moved the skin of paint would be broken, the head fall bodily out from the frame.

At this point of the council a brilliant thought occurred to Tommy. 'Why should not the enjoyment be doubled, and the musical instruments and family pictures of both establishments be sacrificed on the altar of pleasure?' This was agreed to *nem. con.*; and then the meeting adjourned for dinner. When they next met it was evident that there was a screw loose somewhere–that there was 'something rotten in the state of Denmark'. After a little fencing on both sides, it came out that all the schemes of domestic reform had been foiled by maternal vigilance, and that so sharp had been the reprimand consequent on a partial discovery of the schemes that they would have to be abandoned–till such time, at least, as increased physical strength would allow the reformers to laugh to scorn parental threats and injunctions.

Sadly the two forlorn youths took out their knives and regarded them; sadly, sadly they thought, as erst did Othello, of all the fair chances of honour and triumph and glory gone for ever. They compared knives with almost the fondness of doting parents. There they were–so equal in size and strength and beauty–dimmed by no corrosive rust, tarnished by no stain, and with unbroken edges of the keenness of Saladin's sword.

So like were the knives that but for the initials scratched in the handles neither boy could have been sure which was his own. After a little while they began mutually to brag of the superior excellence of their respective weapons. Tommy insisted that his was the sharper, Harry asserted that his was the stronger of the two. Hotter and hotter grew the war of words. The tempers of Harry and Tommy got inflamed, and their boyish bosoms glowed with manly thoughts of daring and hate. But there was abroad in that hour a spirit of a bygone age–one that penetrated even to that dim arbour in the grove of Bubb. The world-old scheme of ordeal was whispered by the spirit in the ear of each, and suddenly the tumult was allayed. With one impulse the boys suggested that they should test the quality of their knives by the ordeal of the Hack.

No sooner said than done. Harry held out his knife edge uppermost; and Tommy, grasping his firmly by the handle, brought down the edge of the blade crosswise on Harry's. The process was then reversed, and Harry became in turn the aggressor. Then they paused and eagerly looked for the result. It was not hard to see; in each knife were two great dents of equal depth; and so it was necessary to renew the contest, and seek a further proof.

What needs it to relate seriatim the details of that direful strife? The sun had long since gone down, and the moon with fair, smiling face had long risen over the roof of Bubb, when, wearied and jaded, Harry and Tommy sought their respective homes. Alas! the splendour of the knives was gone for ever. Ichabod!–Ichabod! the glory had departed and naught remained but two useless wrecks, with keen edges destroyed, and now like unto nothing save the serried hills of Spain.

But though they mourned for their fondly cherished weapons, the hearts of the boys were glad; for the bygone day had opened to their gaze a prospect of pleasure as boundless as the limits of the world.

5

THE FIRST CRUSADE

From that day a new era dawned in the lives of Harry and Tommy. So long as the resources of the parental establishments could hold out so long would their new amusement continue. Subtly they obtained surreptitious possession of articles of family cutlery not in general use, and brought them one by one to their rendezvous. These came fair and spotless from the sanctity of the butler's pantry. Alas! they returned not as they came.

But in course of time the stock of available cutlery became exhausted, and again the inventive faculties of the youths were called into requisition. They reasoned thus: 'The knife game, it is true, is played out, but the excitement of the hack is not to be dispensed with. Let us carry, then, this great idea into new worlds; let us still live in the sunshine of pleasure; let us continue to hack, but with objects other than knives.'

It was done. Not knives now engaged the attention of the ambitious youths. Spoons and forks were daily flattened and beaten out of shape; pepper castor met pepper castor in combat, and both were borne dying from the field; candlesticks met in fray to part no more on this side of the grave; even epergnes were used as weapons in the crusade of hack.

At last all the resources of the butler's pantry became exhausted, and then began a system of miscellaneous destruction that proved in a little time ruinous to the furniture of the respective homes of Harry and Tommy. Mrs Santon and Mrs Merford began to notice that the wear and tear in their households became excessive. Day after day some new domestic calamity seemed to have occurred. Today a valuable edition of some book whose luxurious binding made it an object for public display would appear to have suffered some dire misfortune, for the edges were frayed and broken and the back loose if not altogether displaced; tomorrow the same awful fate would seem to have followed some miniature frame; the day following the legs of some chair or spider-table would show signs of extraordinary hardship. Even in the nursery the sounds of lamentation were heard. It was a thing of daily occurrence for the little girls to state that when going to bed at night they had laid their dear dollies in their beds with tender care, but that when again seeking them in the period of recess they had found them with all their beauty gone, with legs and arms amputated and faces beaten from all semblance of human form.

Then articles of crockery began to be missed. The thief could in no case be discovered, and the wages of the servants, from constant stoppages, began to be nominal rather than real. Mrs Merford and Mrs Santon mourned their losses, but

Harry and Tommy gloated day after day over their spoils, which lay in an ever-increasing heap in the hidden grove of Bubb. To such an extent had the fondness of the hack now grown that with both youths it was an infatuation–a madness–a frenzy.

At length one awful day arrived. The butlers of the houses of Merford and Santon, harassed by constant losses and complaints, and finding that their breakage account was in excess of their wages, determined to seek some sphere of occupation where, if they did not meet with a suitable reward or recognition of their services, they would, at least, not lose whatever fortune and reputation they had already acquired. Accordingly, before rendering up their keys and the goods entrusted to their charge, they proceeded to take a preliminary stock of their own accounts, to make sure of their accredited accuracy. Dire indeed was their distress when they knew to the full the havoc which had been wrought; terrible their anguish of the present, bitter their thoughts of the future. Their hearts, bowed down with weight of woe, failed them quite; reeled the strong brains that had erst overcome foes of deadlier spirit than grief; and fell their stalwart forms prone on the floors of their respective sancta sanctorum.

Late in the day when their services were required they were sought for in bower and hall, and at length discovered where they lay.

But alas for justice! They were accused of being drunk and for having, whilst in that degraded condition, deliberately injured all the property on which they could lay hands. Were not the evidences of their guilt patent to all in the hecatombs of the destroyed? Then they were charged with all the evils wrought in the houses, and on their indignant denial Harry and Tommy, each in his own home, according to their concerted scheme of action, stepped forward and relieved their minds of the deadly weight that had for long in secret borne them down. The story of each ran that time after time he had seen the butler, when he thought that nobody was looking, knocking knives together in the pantry, chairs and books and pictures in the drawing-room and study, dolls in the nursery, and plates in the kitchen. Then, indeed, was the master of each household stern and uncompromising in his demands for justice. Each butler was committed to the charge of myrmidons of the law under the double charge of drunkenness and wilful destruction of property.

Softly and sweetly slept Harry and Tommy in their little beds that night. Angels seemed to whisper to them, for they smiled as though lost in pleasant dreams. The rewards given by proud and grateful parents lay in their pockets, and in their hearts the happy consciousness of having done their duty.

Truly sweet should be the slumbers of the just.

6

'LET THE DEAD PAST BURY ITS DEAD'

It might be supposed that now the operations of Harry and Tommy would be obliged to be abandoned.

Not so, however. The minds of these youths were of no common order, nor were their souls of such weak nature as to yield at the first summons of necessity. Like Nelson, they knew not fear; like Napoleon, they held 'impossible' to be the adjective of fools; and they revelled in the glorious truth that in the lexicon of youth is no such word as 'fail'. Therefore on the day following the *éclaircissement* of the butlers' misdeeds, they met in the arbour to plan a new campaign.

In the hour when all seemed blackest to them, and when the narrowing walls of possibility hedged them in on every side, thus ran the deliberations of these dauntless youths: 'We have played out the meaner things that are inanimate and inert; why not then trench on the domains of life? The dead have lapsed into the regions of the forgotten past–let the living look to themselves.'

That night they met when all households had retired to balmy sleep, and naught but the amorous wailings of nocturnal cats told of the existence of life and sentience. Each bore into the arbour in his arms a pet rabbit and a piece of sticking-plaster. Then, in the peaceful, quiet moonlight, commenced a work of mystery, blood, and gloom. The proceedings began by the fixing of a piece of sticking-plaster over the mouth of each rabbit to prevent it making a noise, if so inclined. Then Tommy held up his rabbit by its scutty tail, and it hung wriggling, a white mass in the moonlight. Slowly Harry raised his rabbit holding it in the same manner, and when level with his head brought it down on Tommy's client.

But the chances had been miscalculated. The boys held firmly to the tails, but the chief portions of the rabbits fell to earth. Ere the doomed beasts could escape, however, the operators had pounced upon them, and this time holding them by the hind legs renewed the trial.

Deep into the night the game was kept up, and the eastern sky began to show signs of approaching day as each boy bore triumphantly the dead corse of his favourite bunny and placed it within its sometime hutch.

Next night the same game was renewed with a new rabbit on each side, and for more than a week–so long as the hutches supplied the wherewithal–the battle was sustained. True that there were sad hearts and red eyes in the juveniles of Santon and Merford as one by one the beloved pets were found dead, but Harry and Tommy, with the hearts of heroes steeled to suffering and deaf to the pitiful cries of childhood, still fought the good fight on to the bitter end.

When the supply of rabbits was exhausted, other munition was not wanting, and for some days the war was continued with white mice, dormice, hedgehogs, guinea pigs, pigeons, lambs, canaries, parakeets, linnets, squirrels, parrots, marmots, poodles, ravens, tortoises, terriers, and cats. Of these, as might be expected, the most difficult to manipulate were the terriers and the cats, and of these two classes the proportion of the difficulties in the way of terrier-hacking was, when compared with those of cat-hacking, about that which the simple lac of the British pharmacopoeia bears to water in the compound which dairymen palm off upon a too-confiding public as milk. More than once when engaged in the rapturous delights of cat-hacking had Harry and Tommy wished that the silent tomb could ope its ponderous and massy jaws and engulf them, for the feline victims were not patient in their death agonies, and often broke the bonds in which the security of the artists rested, and turned fiercely on their executioners.

At last, however, all the animals available were sacrificed; but the passion for hacking still remained. How was it all to end?

A CLOUD WITH GOLDEN LINING

Tommy and Harry sat in the arbour dejected and disconsolate. They wept like two Alexanders because there were no more worlds to conquer. At last the conviction had been forced upon them that the resources available for hacking were exhausted. That very morning they had had a desperate battle, and their attire showed the ravages of direful war. Their hats were battered into shapeless masses, their shoes were soleless and heel-less and had the uppers broken, the ends of their braces, their sleeves, and their trousers were frayed, and had they indulged in the manly luxury of coat-tails these too would have gone.

Truly, hacking had become an absorbing passion with them. Long and fiercely had they been swept onwards on the wings of the demon of strife, and powerless at the best of times had been the promptings of good; but now, heated with combat, maddened by the equal success of arms, and with the lust for victory still unsated, they longed more fiercely than ever for some new pleasure: like tigers that have tasted blood they thirsted for a larger and more potent libation.

As they sat, with their souls in a tumult of desire and despair, some evil genius guided into the garden the twin blossoms of the tree of Bubb. Hand in hand Zacariah and Zerubbabel advanced from the back door; they had escaped from their nurses, and with the exploring instinct of humanity, advanced boldly into the great world–the *terra incognita*, the *ultima Thule* of the paternal domain.

In the course of time they approached the hedge of poplars, from behind which the anxious eyes of Harry and Tommy looked for their approach, for the boys knew that where the twins were the nurses were accustomed to be gathered together, and they feared discovery if their retreat should be cut off.

It was a touching sight, these lovely babes, alike in form, feature, size, expression, and dress; in fact, so like each other that one 'might not have told either from which'. When the startling similarity was recognized by Harry and Tommy, each suddenly turned, and, grasping the other by the shoulder, spoke in a keen whisper: 'Hack! They are exactly equal! This is the very apotheosis of our art!'

With excited faces and trembling hands they laid their plans to lure the unsuspecting babes within the precincts of their charnel house, and they were so successful in their efforts that in a little time the twins had toddled behind the hedge and were lost to the sight of the parental mansion.

Harry and Tommy were not famed for gendeness within the immediate precincts of their respective homes, but it would have delighted the heart of any philanthropist to see the kindly manner in which they arranged for the pleasures of the helpless babes. With smiling faces and playful words and gentle wiles they led them within the arbour, and then, under pretence of giving them some of those sudden jumps in which infants rejoice, they raised them from the ground. Tommy held Zacariah across his arm with his baby moon-face smiling up at the cobwebs on the arbour roof, and Harry, with a mighty effort, raised the cherubic Zerubbabel aloft.

Each nerved himself for a great endeavour, Harry to give, Tommy to endure a shock, and then the form of Zerubbabel was seen whirling through the air round Harry's glowing and determined face. There was a sickening crash and the arm of Tommy yielded visibly.

The pasty face of Zerubbabel had fallen fair on that of Zacariah, for Tommy and Harry were by this time artists of too great experience to miss so simple a mark. The putty-like noses collapsed, the puttylike cheeks became for a moment flattened, and when in an instant more they parted, the faces of both were dabbled in gore. Immediately the firmament was rent with a series of such yells as might have awakened the dead. Forthwith from the house of Bubb came the echoes in parental cries and footsteps. As the sounds of scurrying feet rang through the mansion, Harry cried to Tommy: 'They will be on us soon. Let us cut to the roof of the stable and draw up the ladder.'

Tommy answered by a nod, and the two boys, regardless of consequences, and bearing each a twin, ascended to the roof of the stable by means of a ladder which usually stood against the wall, and which they pulled up after them.

As Ephraim Bubb issued from his house in pursuit of his lost darlings, the sight which met his gaze froze his very soul. There, on the coping of the stable roof, stood Harry and Tommy renewing their game. They seemed like two young demons forging some diabolical implement, for each in turn the twins were lifted high in air and let fall with stunning force on the supine form of its fellow. How Ephraim felt none but a tender and imaginative father can conceive. It would be enough to wring the heart of even a callous parent to see his children, the darlings of his old age—his own beloved twins—being sacrificed to the brutal pleasure of unregenerate youths, without being made unconsciously and helplessly guilty of the crime of fratricide.

Loudly did Ephraim and also Sophonisba, who, with dishevelled locks, had now appeared upon the scene, bewail their unhappy lot and shriek in vain for aid; but by rare ill-chance no eyes save their own saw the work of butchery or heard the shrieks of anguish and despair. Wildly did Ephraim, mounting on the shoulders of his spouse, strive, but in vain, to scale the stable wall.

Baffled in every effort, he rushed into the house and

appeared in a moment bearing in his hands a double-barrelled gun, into which he poured the contents of a shot pouch as he ran. He came anigh the stable and hailed the murderous youths: 'Drop them twins and come down here or I'll shoot you like a brace of dogs.'

'Never!' exclaimed the heroic two with one impulse, and continued their awful pastime with a zest tenfold as they knew that the agonized eyes of parents wept at the cause of their joy.

'Then die!' shrieked Ephraim, as he fired both barrels, right–left, at the hackers.

But, alas! love for his darlings shook the hand that never shook before. As the smoke cleared off and Ephraim recovered from the kick of his gun, he heard a loud twofold laugh of triumph and saw Harry and Tommy, all unhurt, waving in the air the trunks of the twins–the fond father had blown the heads completely off his own offspring.

Tommy and Harry shrieked aloud in glee, and after playing catch with the bodies for some time, seen only by the agonized eyes of the infanticide and his wife, flung them high in the air. Ephraim leaped forward to catch what had once been Zacariah, and Sophonisba grabbed wildly for the loved remains of her Zerubbabel.

But the weight of the bodies and the height from which they fell were not reckoned by either parent, and from being ignorant of a simple dynamical formula each tried to effect an object which calm, common sense, united with scientific knowledge, would have told them was impossible. The masses fell, and Ephraim and Sophonisba were stricken dead by the falling twins, who were thus posthumously guilty of the crime of parricide.

An intelligent coroner's jury found the parents guilty of the crimes of infanticide and suicide, on the evidence of Harry and Tommy, who swore, reluctantly, that the inhuman monsters, maddened by drink, had killed their offspring by shooting them into the air out of a cannon –since stolen– whence like curses they had fallen on their own heads; and that then they had slain themselves *suis manibus* with their own hands.

Accordingly Ephraim and Sophonisba were denied the solace of Christian burial, and were committed to the earth with 'maimed rites', and had stakes driven through their middles to pin them down in their unhallowed graves till the crack of doom.

Harry and Tommy were each rewarded with national honours and were knighted, even at their tender years.

Fortune seemed to smile upon them all the long after-years, and they lived to a ripe old age, hale of body, and respected and beloved of all.

Often in the golden summer eves, when all nature seemed

at rest, when the oldest cask was opened and the largest lamp was lit, when the chestnuts glowed in the embers and the kid turned on the spit, when their great-grandchildren pretended to mend fictional armour and to trim an imaginary helmet's plume, when the shuttles of the good wives of their grandchildren went flashing each through its proper loom, with shouting and with laughter they were accustomed to tell the tale of THE DUALITISTS; OR, THE DEATH DOOM OF THE DOUBLE BORN.

J. M. SYNGE

Edmund John Millington Synge was born in County Dublin, Ireland in 1871. He started violin lessons at the age of sixteen, and entered Trinity College, Dublin in 1888, where he studied Gaelic and Irish antiquities. After gradating, he spent time living in the Black Forest and Germany, where he began to write plays and poetry. In 1892, with the aim of making art accessible to the common man, Synge founded the Irish Literary Society. Four years later, in Pairs, he met W. B. Yeats, with whom he maintained a lifelong friendship.

On the advice of Yeats, whom he asked for help in finding his poetic voice, Synge began to travel extensively around the Aran Islands, living with peasant seaman, practicing his Gaelic and absorbing the local history and folklore.In 1903, Synge returned to London with two one-act plays, *Riders to the Sea* and *The Shadow of the Glen*. Both were performed over the following few years, and remain popular to this day, despite the controversy they initially ignited amongst Irish nationalists. In 1904, Synge was appointed literary advisor to the newly opened Abbey Theatre, and soon became one of the directors of the company, along with Yeats.

Three years on, *The Playboy of the Western World*—widely regarded as Synge's masterpiece—was performed.Its portrayal of the Irish sparked riots in Dublin, much to Sygne's horror.

In 1908 and 1910 respectively, he published his two final works, *The Tinkers Wedding* and *Deirdre of the Sorrows*. Synge died in Dublin in 1909, aged just 37.

JOSEPH SHERIDAN LE FANU

Joseph Thomas Sheridan Le Fanu was born in Dublin in 1814. His was a literary family of Huguenot origins; both his grandmother Alicia Sheridan Le Fanu and his great-uncle Richard Brinsley Sheridan were playwrights, and his niece Rhoda Broughton would go on to become a successful novelist. Le Fanu's family lived in a variety of locations around rural Ireland during his youth–the folk superstitions of which are said to have left a deep impression on him–and were financially hard-hit by the agitations of the Tithe Wars. In 1833, not long after the death of his father, Le Fanu entered Trinity College, Dublin to study law. While there, he was elected Auditor of the College Historical Society, and between 1838 and 1840 published his first series of short stories, which were later collected as *The Purcell Papers*.

Le Fanu was called to the bar in 1839, but he never practiced and soon abandoned law for journalism. During the 1840s, he married, and spent time mounting a protest against the indifference of the government to the Irish Famine. He also produced his first two novels–*The Cock and Anchor* (1845) and *The Fortunes of Colonel Torlogh O'Brien* (1847); both works of historical fiction–and in 1851 he and his wife Susanna moved to their house on Merrion Square, Dublin, where le Fanu was to remain until his death. In 1858,

Le Fanu's wife Susanna died in unclear circumstances, and he became a recluse, setting to work in his most productive and successful years as a writer. Between 1864 and 1872, he produced ten novels, all in the 'sensation fiction' genre popular at the time.

At his peak, le Fanu was the leading ghost-story writer of the nineteenth century, and he is now seen as central to the development of the genre in the Victorian era. His work is credited with turning the Gothic's focus from the external sources of horror to the inward effects of terror, thus helping to create the psychological basis for supernaturalist literature that continues to this day. Arguably le Fanu's most enduring works are *Uncle Silas*, published in 1864, and the vampire novella *Camilla* (1872), which influenced Bram Stoker in the writing of *Dracula* and has inspired several films. Le Fanu died in his native Dublin in 1873, at the age of 58.

LADY WILDE

Lady Wilde was born Jane Francesca Elgee in Dublin in 1821. During her life, she was a staunch Irish nationalist, and began publishing poetry during the 1840s in *The Nation*, under the pseudonym 'Speranza'. Much of her work was Pro-Irish and anti-British; when she wrote commentary calling for armed revolution in Ireland, the British authorities at Dublin Castle shut down the paper. In 1854, Wilde gave birth to her son, Oscar, who went on become one of the best-known authors of the nineteenth century. In later life, she supplemented her income by writing for fashionable magazines, and collecting and publishing Irish fairy tales. Lady Wilde contracted bronchitis in January of 1896 and, dying, asked for permission to see Oscar, who was in prison on charges of "gross indecency with other men." Her request was refused. She died at her home a month later, aged 74.

BRAM STOKER

Abraham 'Bram' Stoker was born in Dublin, Ireland in 1847. Stoker was a semi-invalid as a child, and was bedridden until he started school at the age of seven. However, he made a full recovery and went on to excel as an athlete at Trinity College, which he enrolled at in 1864. Stoker graduated with honours in mathematics in 1870, and was also president of the university's philosophical society.

Stoker developed an interest in theatre, and became theatre critic for the *Dublin Evening Mail* in his early twenties. It was following a favourable review he gave of an 1876 Henry Irving production of *Hamlet* that Stoker and Irving struck up a friendship. Three years later, in the same year that Stoker married Florence Balcombe (whose former suitor was Oscar Wilde), he became acting-manager and then business manager of Irving's Lyceum Theatre—a post he went on to hold for 27 years. As a result of his close friendship with Irving (the most famous actor of his day), Stoker became something of a socialite. He mingled with London's high society, meeting writers such as Sir Arthur Conan Doyle, and travelled extensively in the United States, where he spent time with both Theodore Roosevelt and Walt Whitman.

While working for Irving, Stoker began to write novels, eventually producing a total of fifteen works of fiction.

Although most met with at least mild success, Stoker is best known for his 1897 publication, *Dracula*. This work–an epistolary novel weaving hypnotism, magic, the supernatural, and other elements of Gothic fiction–went on to sell over one million copies, and has never been out of print. Today, the novel and its eponymous protagonist remain so well-known that one can actually visit the castle of Count Dracula in the Transylvanian region of Romania–despite the fact that Stoker never even went there himself.

After a series of strokes, Stoker died in London in 1912, aged 64.

ST. JOHN D. SEYMOUR

St. John Drelincourt Seymour was born in the second half of the 19th century in Ireland. Around 1913, he came to realize that although Ireland was replete with collections of folklore and fairy-tales, the country's rich tradition of ghost stories remained largely untapped. Working with friend Harry L. Neligan, Seymour set out to correct this. The two of them put out a request for anecdotes in the newspapers of the day, and compiled the stories they received in what is now Seymour's most well-known 'non-fiction' work, *True Irish Ghost Stories* (1914). Around the same time, Seymour published his other more popular titles, *Irish Witchcraft and Demonology* and *Haunted Houses in or Near Dublin*.